"It's ticking."

Five minutes later, Caulfield was standing back in the tram, looking down at the offending rucksack.

He got on the phone straightaway.

"It has a label on the side," he reported to the Bomb Squad. It read, 'Rucksack Rebels'. "It's not The Rucksack Raiders. Maybe it's a different group. What do you think?"

"We're not going to get there in time," the Sergeant told him. "You need to grab it and heft it into the river. Don't make a fuss, just do it. You can't take the chance and wait. It's not an option."

Caulfield looked around. Pomona Station was built up on pillars, so that it was level with the bridge. It was ten metres up in the air. Behind him, the tram door was open and beyond the platform fence there was open air and an abrupt drop. He took a deep breath.

He was thinking, I can do this. I am here. No one else is.

I need to act.

Cover photo: Mike Scantlebury

Other books by this author:

are available
(in the Mickey from Manchester series).

Also, Amelia Hartliss Mysteries, the series.

*(A full list of other publications
is at the back of this book.)*

JC's Cure for Cancer

A Crime Fiction Thriller

by

Mike Scantlebury

The Amelia Hartliss Mysteries series, Book 17

Published in Britain the year the President visited
2018

Copyright
(Yes, really)
Copyright © 2018 by Mike Scantlebury

First Printing: 2018
ISBN   978-1-9808-1634-8

Publishing by Amazon.com on the orders
of Mike Scantlebury,
an indie author and publisher, now based
in Salford Free Town, UK

www.Salford.me

Ordering Information:
This book is available online at all good online bookstores and also at High Street
bookstores where you can walk in, ask for it and place an order.

Dedication

Thanks to Lulu.com, a self-processed print on demand
publisher, that helped to publish a book about
cures for cancer.
Those are the stories that inspired me.

Unfortunately, all I could come up with
was a tale of mystery and intrigue.
Listen, I'm not suggesting I have answers.
No, this story here is about possibilities.
What would happen if someone did find a cure?
How would it be received?

What do you think?
Would people be willing to believe the good news?

Or would there simply be even more confusion
and bad feeling than there already is?

Contents

1. CHAPTER ONE: Church and State......................................7

2. CHAPTER TWO: Secrets of The Big Top......................21

3. CHAPTER THREE: Scars of the past...........................35

4. CHAPTER FOUR: Always the hero 49

5. CHAPTER FIVE: Fakes..63

6. CHAPTER SIX: Mistaken Identity................................75

7. CHAPTER SEVEN: Misunderstandings 88

8. CHAPTER EIGHT: Ruthless..102

9. CHAPTER NINE: News and Goodbyes 116

10. CHAPTER TEN: A place in the sun 129

11. THE END..145

12. ABOUT THE AUTHOR 147

Other Books by Mike Scantlebury..................................149

2.   CHAPTER ONE: Church and State

The Vicar was baffled by the attractive young woman sitting opposite her.

"Most people call me Melia," the young woman said.

The priest didn't doubt that, but the rest didn't match up to the usual look of an aspiring volunteer for the church.

She was far too attractive.

The young lady had striking auburn hair falling over her shoulders and framing a pretty face. She was dressed in a tight-fitting leather jacket, concealing a full figure in a figure-hugging thin sweater. She wore worn jeans, supported by a thick leather belt, and her feet were covered in high leather boots. She looked like she belonged in America's Old West, taming cowboys in a frontier town, shooting six guns and wielding a long whip.

She probably carries a gun, the Vicar was thinking.

Thoughtfully, the priest said: "I served twelve years in the Army before I took up this local calling."

The girl called Melia stared back, meeting the older woman's gaze.

Making up her mind, she reached over and offered her hand. The handshake was firm, but the fingers were delicate.

"Special Forces?" Melia asked, recognising the secret grip.

"What about you? I'm guessing British Security. Maybe - what is it called now - WSB?"

Melia broke out into a massive grin.

"That's what we used to be," she laughed. "But we move with the times. We've been renamed TEEF - Total

Environment Energy Force. We still cover the country, and our main focus remains anti-terrorism."

The middle-aged Vicar nodded. She was older now, slightly over-weight, but she had clashed with 'Security' in her years in the Service, and didn't take their interest lightly. So, why would they bother visiting her suburban church?

"I'm guessing I can trust you," Melia said, "so I'll give you the background if you're happy to keep quiet about it."

The Vicar, Ms Karney, nodded. It was a bother. She was hoping it wasn't going to stifle her project.

Melia said: "You take in homeless people when the weather gets cold. Like now, we've got Siberian winds from the east and Storm Emma from Southern Europe. It's some of the coldest nights that Salford has ever seen."

"It's unbearable in Manchester city centre," the Vicar agreed, "so some of the people cross the river and look for shelter in places like this. I thought you were here for that - to help. We need volunteers, every one we can get."

"Oh, I'm up for that," Melia agreed. "I've had years of experience of putting up camp beds and cooking for a squad. No problem there. Still, while all that's going on - and if you don't mind - I'll be scanning the faces."

Melia reached in to the inner pocket of her jacket and pulled out a small, black and white photograph.

"This is the man I'm looking for," she told the priest.

"What's he done?"

"Honestly, we don't know. What we do know is that he's been out of the country for four years and the story his family tells is that he was aiming to go to the Middle East. They suspect he's been fighting, maybe Syria. Maybe Iraq."

The priest sighed. "It seems a pity you're trying to collar him. He might have been on the side of the good guys."

"I don't make the rules," Melia said uneasily. Yes, she knew there was a bit of a problem there. She was being asked to apprehend the man, simply because he had returned to the UK. She would then hand him over and he would be questioned. Yes, it might seem unjust if it was discovered he had been fighting *against* terrorists, (the same job she was doing), but Melia didn't allow herself to get bogged down in politics and didn't want to think about the details.

The law was clear: you couldn't leave Britain, fight abroad and hope to come back when it suited you, as if nothing had happened. Unfortunately, it meant you would have drawn attention to yourself, and you would have to answer questions.

Melia wanted to sigh too. It was ironic. People she knew - and, probably, people the Vicar once knew, in the Army - did exactly that, turning themselves into mercenaries and soldiers of fortune. For them, they could avoid the spotlight. The people who got caught were mostly young, mostly immature, mostly very, very bad at fighting.

Just like the kid in the photo. A hopeless amateur.

The Vicar put the photo on the table and watched Melia scoop it up. Oh well, the priest was thinking. I do need helpers.

"I'll show you round," she said. "The rough sleepers aren't allowed in until seven at the earliest, which give us just four hours from now to get everything set up and ready. I could do with an extra pair of hands making the beds."

It was a church. The campbeds were in a cupboard under the balcony. The blankets were in drawers. Most days of the week, and all weekends, the place was used by worshippers and groups from the community. At that moment, there were Mums and toddlers playing in the back room. The Vicar had been talking to Melia in her office, a small room near the front door. She was about to lead the younger girl out when the phone rang.

She had to pick it up. It could be an Emergency, she was thinking.

It was. Someone was dying.

Melia was still sitting in the chair across the desk from her interviewer. She didn't know whether to stand, or wait. She had secured her first objective - getting accepted in the church - and was happy to move on, doing whatever was needed to feed and provide bed places for a dozen homeless people. It was a good cause. She was happy to help.

The Reverend Karney was growing increasingly agitated. Her voice was rising, in pitch and mood.

"No, he is NOT here," she snapped. "I don't know where he is. He should never have given you this number! It's completely unacceptable. Yes, I know what you would have read online. Jeremy does that. He works online. No, he doesn't work here. He comes to our Monday morning group, that's all. I can't tell you any more. Really."

Melia found herself becoming concerned. She had only just met this older woman, but she felt confidence in her. She seemed to know what was right, what was needed. Why was she being harassed? It sounded awful.

"No, do NOT get on a plane!" the priest insisted. "He can't help you. It's not real. Yes, that is my opinion."

She was shaking when she put down the phone. There seemed to be tears in her eyes.

Melia did the only thing she knew how to do - she walked round the desk and put her arms around the other's shoulders. She held her tight, as she had held her colleagues when things went wrong and there was nothing else to do.

The priest, on the verge of tears, didn't actually cry. If anything, she seemed to be getting angry.

"Irresponsible!" she snapped. "Completely irresponsible. He has no right to be saying these things."

Melia guessed it had nothing to do with the Homelessness Project. This was something completely different.

Perhaps that was why the Vicar was so upset. She needed to be focussing on the homeless and was being distracted.

"Maybe tonight," the priest said unsteadily. "In the coldness and dark of the early hours, I'll tell you the whole story. A parishioner, a member of the congregation, is a trained engineer. He believes he has found a device, a concoction of wires and probes, that has miraculous properties. It can do all sorts of magical things. It can heal and repair."

Melia looked interested. Something new? An invention?

The Vicar explained: "Jeremy says it can cure cancer."

They both looked at each other, weighing that up, thinking through the ramifications.

But the priest really was annoyed. "That call was from a man in Texas," she stormed. "He said he had read Jeremy's web page. He wanted to know if I could 'verify' the claims - if I could 'guarantee' a cure! I said I couldn't. He said he was 'prepared to get on the next plane'. I can't have that. I can't have invaders from all around the world - "

She was lost for words. Horror and concern flooded her face and she looked about to explode.

It was a poignant moment for Melia.

She could have told her new 'employer', if they had known each other well enough, that yes, most people called her Melia, but her given name was Amelia Hartliss, and her friends, as well as a few enemies, liked to call her 'Heartless'. It was a good joke, and mostly, quite appropriate. When she was busy, doing her job, Melia had no time for unnecessary emotions. She was a consummate professional, able to concentrate on the job in hand, doing what needed to be done.

But here, now, in this struggling, small church, in a suburb that was deprived and in need of regeneration, Melia felt herself overwhelmed by surges of unexpected doubt, fear and despair. People with cancer, facing death, were willing to fly half way across the planet in search of treatment? What a horrible position to be in.

Melia, 'Heartless' to the world, found herself strangely moved.

* * * * *

Meanwhile, Melia's boss, Captain Gibson, was a mile away across Salford at that particular moment, at home.

That is, the place the Captain called 'home' while he was in Salford. Originally from London, he still had a house down there, but he hadn't cared to live in it after his wife died. He found himself spending more and more time 'up north'. The Agency had been forced to find him somewhere. At first they had been happy to put him up in a local hotel, but the bills were mounting and the Unit was being hounded to save money from somewhere in the budget, so Human Resources suggested an Executive Interim arrangement. Gibson had never heard of it, but it was increasingly popular after the BBC moved some of its departments out of the capital and into the new base at Salford Quays.

In effect, what it amounted to was a wooden house.

Gibson, having spent some years in the Royal Engineers during his time in the Army, admired its solid construction and its practicality. The design was based on a plan from the 1950s dreamt up by German architect Walter Siegel, and involved a square frame of timbers, filled in with heavily insulated panels.

The windows were large and triple glazed, which gave the rooms an incredibly light and airy feel. A local entrepreneur had seen the attraction for people moving up from London, or other places. They needed, above all, space, plenty of room for all their goods and furniture which was being transferred. They might arrive as a single but might later need accommodation for a spouse and probably family, bit by bit, as the move progressed. It was good that the houses were so spacious and adaptable, and a generally better alternative to hotel rooms or cramped flats or other apartments.

The clientele was always on the move, of course, as more permanent arrangements were made. Gibson, on the other hand, had been in the same house for four years. It hadn't made him happy. It simply reminded him of the impermanence of his base. There were unpacked boxes in side rooms and suitcases containing things he had never looked at. Now, in contemplative mode, he had started sorting. It wasn't making him any happier.

He found photo albums from his Service career. Seeing grinning faces in dusty desert camps made him nostalgic about his early days as a soldier. Then he thought of how few of those people were still alive, and that simply made him depressed. Sitting in a comfortable chair, clothes and boxes scattered around him, he wasn't feeling great.

My time has come, he was thinking.

In the first instance, he needed to retire. He had been saying that for years, and once, a while ago, he had actually moved out of his office, but then an emergency struck and he was called back. It can't go on for ever, he realised. They will dump me eventually. Then I will need to move to the countryside and tend some roses, or something.

The regret that was making him most gloomy, was that he hadn't been able to choose his successor.

For years, he had thought - and most of his team had agreed with him - that Mickey would be the obvious person to take on the job of Director. But Mickey wasn't having it. The big man had said, instead, that he wanted to 'scale back' his involvement. He was never committed to WSB, he reminded people. He had retired from the Army, secure on his pension, and had planned a quiet life at his house in North Salford. Mickey was still 'on call' of course, a valuable asset that the government would never let go, and he had been 'attached' to WSB and seen a host of actions in recent years.

Gibson hated that he couldn't simply transfer responsibility into a 'safe pair of hands', as he knew Mickey was.

Then there was the name. It stopped being WSB the day that Regional Office in Salford burned down. It wasn't a coincidence, that fire - it was enemy action. The Unit had cast around for a new base, then settled on premises actually in Salford Quays. It was central, good transport connections and near the BBC. The team had hardly settled in yet, and there were teething troubles with the facilities, but the name had gone. Gibson was fuming. Something to do with 'teeth'. What idiot in London had come up with such a foolish proposition?

Gibson opened another case. The garish purple paraphernalia shocked him. God, I haven't worn those robes for ages, he was thinking. But what's the point? He had joined The Sacred Society at an early point in his career, and it had helped him climb the ladder. Most officers were members. He knew the rituals and attended all the dinners. It was nonsense, he decided. Maybe the fact he had been so negative about all the routines and handshakes, maybe that's what lost him approval in the higher echelons. Perhaps that was why he couldn't count on their support these days.

Then another case, and this was family snaps, pictures of holidays and time playing with the kids in the garden. His wife looked so vibrant, so full of life. Amazing that she been struck down so young.

And the children. Valerie, who died shortly before his wife, in a drowning incident. It had affected both of them so badly, and nearly ended their marriage. Their son - he had never been the same. Still a teenager, and losing first his sister and then his mother, it ruined him. He went completely off the rails, left home, travelled and never communicated. Strange, Gibson was thinking. People often say I treat Mickey like my son, but he isn't my son. David is. Where he lives now, what he's doing, Gibson had no idea. Perhaps I'd better get in touch, he was thinking, before the end.

Gibson stood up, went over to the window. He caught sight of his reflection in the glass. Instead of the usual immaculate suit, he was in pyjama bottoms and a rough shirt, open to the navel, barely covered by a dressing gown. He looked old, decrepit, like a Grandfather abandoned in an Old People's Home, after he could no longer look after himself.

His hair was awry, flopping over to one side, instead of being carefully combed, and his chin was stubbly, since he hadn't bothered with his regular daily shave. He wasn't looking after himself, he realised.

He looked out on to the industrial landscape. Is this it? he wondered. Do I have to end my days in this desert of dereliction? Will anybody within fifty miles mourn my passing?

Because that was it. That was the real cause of all his distress. Gibson was dying, and he knew it.

Over on the low coffee table behind the man, there was a brown envelope with a hospital stamp on it. Inside was a list of the mixed results of recent tests. They were contradictory, the Consultant had told the old man, but their summation was very clear: the Captain had a limited time to live. It might be years, the doctor said, but it could be months.

Either way, Gibson was advised to 'put his affairs in order' and make peace with himself. He didn't have long.

I wonder, Gibson mused to himself, if Melia would be willing to take the reins? She's young, but she's very capable. Everyone in the office looks up to her. Some worship her, like Terry the technician. He would gladly call her 'Boss'.

Perhaps I'll suggest that, the Captain decided. Yes, I'll definitely bring it up at the next Executive meeting.

*   *   *   *   *

At the same time, early evening, Deputy Director Caulfield was riding a bus into Manchester.

Caulfield was fuming. He hadn't got over the slight of being passed over. Why wasn't he good enough to be Director? He had been Deputy for several years, and many people might have assumed he would simply move up into the top slot if the Old Man retired. But, No. Gibson had made it very clear to his assistant that it was never going to happen.

It's because I'm a foreigner, Caulfield was thinking, furiously. Discrimination? Of course it is!

Richard Caulfield had been born in England, spending his early years in East Anglia, but then his father had been offered a placement at a University in Eastern Australia, and the whole family upped sticks and moved to the other side of the world. Richard's father had enjoyed a distinguished career, writing several books on diplomacy that were admired world-wide. But young Richard, angry at his dad for taking him out of school where he was happy and depositing him into a melange of education where people couldn't even talk properly, suppressed a continuing rage until he got to an age where he could leave the family home and never return. He didn't even send Christmas cards.

He pitched up in Hong Kong. After some years in retail, he traded in the few qualifications he had to his name and enlisted in the police force. Being a bright lad, intelligent as well as resentful, he found himself being promoted and admired, if only for his professionalism, rather than his personality. He did well, and was happy that when Britain handed the colony back to China in 1997, the British government was able to offer some of its most devoted citizens a lifeline back to the home country. Caulfield filled in the forms, bit the bullet and found himself back in Blighty.

The next few years were undistinguished, but Richard was in London, and found, quite by chance, that he was mixing with people in the higher ranks of the Civil Service. It was a surprise. He'd always thought, based on his Hong Kong years, that only gentlemen in The Sacred Society were allowed into the hallowed halls, but he found himself strangely welcomed, feted and involved. Little did he know that he was being set up. A mandarin in the Home Office arranged a meeting, Caulfield passed the audition, and found himself being offered the role of Deputy Director in a government agency he'd never even heard of. Little did he know that he was a pawn in a complex game of chess, which sprang from a small cabal of bitter men anxious to teach 'the great Captain Gibson' a lesson. They succeeded. They landed Gibson with a hopeless amateur as his titular 'Deputy'. They hoped it would hobble Gibson and ruin his track record of achievement.

The plan nearly worked, but what the conspirators didn't realise was that the Captain had surrounded himself with a team of first-rate detectives and agents, who were adept at plucking the fat from the fire, snatching victory from the jaws of defeat. Gibson, despite the ball and chain around his leg, given to him by his adversaries, didn't fail. His unit kept coming up with the goods, and this was based - in no small measure - on the skills of people like Mickey and Melia.

Caulfield, dumb and blatheringly aggressive, was still smart enough to see who was doing the work. Most of his day-to-day strategy was based on the idea of keeping out of the way of the clever people, so that they'd be free to get on with the job. He would be on-hand, of course, to pick up the credit, once the task was completed.

Something had gone wrong. There was a problem on the buses and Caulfield couldn't find anyone to tackle it. He'd been forced, for one rare time, to get out from behind his desk and take some action in the field.

Caulfield looked around. Nothing suspicious. For most of the day he had been sitting on a succession of seats, riding the number 50 bus into Manchester, then back out again. It was not random. This route linked the main campus of Salford University and the other buildings on Salford Quays. The buses carried students, lots of them, as well as BBC executives and other media people. It was the ideal place for a spot of terrorism, his information told him.

The problem was, Caulfield came to realise, that students in large numbers are noisy, self-obsessed and careless. They were interested in listening to music on their headphones and staring at their mobile phones. Other people, it seemed, mostly got in their way, but they'd happily barge them aside, taking whatever seats were available. Caulfield, older and less resilient, was finding he got bounced backwards and forwards, and was often made to stand, (despite his advancing years). These kids, he was thinking, they are the future of the country? Heaven help us!

Besides, he stood out like a sore thumb. With his regular Italian suit, he looked nothing like a student, or even the kind of aged academic that taught them things. He had the air of a fading gigolo, and the attitude of passive aggression that comes to all that don't achieve their aims in life. He didn't fit in, he realised. Here, or anywhere else.

Caulfield, bored and resentful, was looking forward to the return trip, back to Salford Quays, and then - hopefully - a return to his office. He had started the day late and felt duty bound to put in a few more hours in Regional Office before calling it a day. Yes, he would need to do that. People would notice, he was sure, if he was never around the place. He needed to put in an appearance. It was all about appearances.

There was sudden consternation behind him. Young people were gabbling.

"I don't know what it is," one young man was saying.

"Well, somebody must have left it," a young lady told him.

"It's a rucksack," another voice added. "What do you think it is - a bomb?"

Caulfield leapt to his feet. This is it! he realised. This is what I've been looking for.

"Stop the bus!" he yelled at the driver. "You, phone the police!" he said to the young lady.

"It's just a bag," the third voice was saying, trying to calm everyone down.

"There's wires poking out!" the first kid said, and nearly fell over himself trying to move away.

Deputy Director Caulfield pulled his I.D. from his pocket and bustled everyone to the front of the vehicle. Then, when the driver slewed to a halt in Quay Street, in front of The Peoples' History Museum, he ordered a quiet and orderly evacuation. The passengers were happy to oblige. Anyway, this was Manchester. They could walk to their city centre destinations from there. The driver killed the engine and stood on the pavement. The bus was quiet.

Mr Caulfield, at the door, making sure no one would even think about getting on, considered the authoritative way he had handled the situation and smiled to himself. Soon, the Bomb Squad would arrive. They would look to him.

I am the Hero of the Hour, he thought proudly.

3. CHAPTER TWO: Secrets of The Big Top

"I'm sorry, Melia. I don't believe you," Caulfield said pompously.

Melia stared at her superior, stupefied.

Who did he think he was? What was giving him such airs and graces? She stirred uneasily in her chair. They were sitting in the Deputy Director's new room in the new Regional Office on Salford Quays. It was a great space. On the next to top floor, it had a huge picture window that looked down on the harbourside, with the blocks that belonged to the BBC laid out to their right and the Irwell Arts Centre directly opposite, on the promontory that had once been the tip of Nine Dock.

A waterside location, far superior to the old back street they had once inhabited, and put up with for so long. The new Unit, with a new name, was going up in the world. Literally.

Caulfield, of course, was riding high. It had been a notable few days, since he identified the first rucksack on that first bus. The next day he found more, then, organising the new team members he was allocated, they located four more. The Press were ecstatic, and though they weren't allowed to mention the Deputy Director by name, the praise was heaped on the head of the man who helmed the operation. It was such a success.

Poor reporters. They weren't being completely misinformed, of course, but the information being shared was not the sum total of the truth. The men and women were being led to believe that a dastardly series of bomb plots was being averted.

They didn't know that the 'bombs' were duds.

It was Richard Caulfield who had realised the significance of 'The Rucksack Rebels'. He had been presented with a clutch of social media chats by his technical director, Terry. The young man couldn't make head or tail of the chatter, but Caulfield saw the debate for what it was. Succinctly, some members of a right-wing Christian terror group were suggesting that they should 'give up' killing people! One of their number had noticed that when they left a home-made bomb at Manchester's International Airport, it had resulted in hours of confusion and panic. The bomb was defused and didn't go off, actually. No one was killed and no one was injured. This was great, an anonymous member suggested. Let's do it again.

Let's plant a rucksack again, that's what they were saying. It didn't matter if it was a bomb or not. If people saw it and suspected an explosive device, the area would be cleared, people would be evacuated, services disrupted and plans abandoned. In a very real sense, it didn't matter if the 'device' was real or not. It would completely interfere with the usual run of business, and that was something every 'terrorist' desired.

Well, most of them. Some enjoyed killing, it seemed, and were horrified to be told they didn't need to blow bodies up anymore. They baulked at the very idea, withdrew their support and went off and founded a splinter group. The 'no bomb' bombers, meanwhile, were fed up of talking too. They left and started their own cabal. They called themselves 'The Rucksack Raiders', and over the next few weeks started leaving worrying-looking bags all over public transport in Greater Manchester. Sometimes the bags were simply bags, but just to keep the Security Services on their toes, the Raiders would add some wires spilling out. It added a modicum of verisimilitude and added to the fear.

Caulfield wasn't afraid. He saw the bag on the bus and knew what it was. He wasn't in any danger, he realised.

In fact, it was Terry who deserved most of the praise. Firstly, for identifying the new conspiracy and secondly for keeping up with the interchanges. It was he who had put the idea to the Deputy Director that he needed to focus on the 50 bus - which is why Caulfield was in that seat - and it was Terry who kept supplying Caulfield with possible targets that he had heard being considered on the internet exchanges.

Caulfield, true to form, had no intention of letting a mere technician take the credit for anything, and kept the plaudits strictly for himself. It was all good, he was thinking. It will help my campaign to secure promotion.

Then, another opportunity fell into his lap.

Captain Gibson, for no apparent reason, confided to his deputy that he was considering Melia for the role of his successor. Caulfield, frantic and bruised, recovered in time to realise that he - as the current Deputy Director - would have to be involved in her appointment and interview.

It would give him such power!

Which was why, that particular afternoon, he was sitting in his office with Melia opposite him, and Melia's file and photos spread out on the desk in front of him. It was all about 'Clearance'. If Melia was to be even thought about for the new post, her record would have had to have been scrutinised with the finest of combs. That would be a job for Human Resources, certainly, the Personnel Office, but it would also involve her immediate superior.

And that was the bitter and twisted Mr Richard Caulfield.

The proud man had already amused himself by pouring scorn on Melia's school record. Then he was gratuitously insulting about her University, since it was far too 'modern' to earn his admiration.

Now he had moved on to more 'personal' matters.

"How long has your affair with Mickey been going on?" he mused, insultingly.

Melia grimaced. If only it had been 'an affair', she was thinking.

In truth it had been an on-off romance that had started when she first arrived in Salford, half a decade ago, but could hardly have been said to have 'continued'. Mickey was infuriating, Melia could have said, (if she had felt confident in confiding in her boss), because she was never sure whether he really cared for her or not. He was forever running off, disappearing, on duties both home and overseas, and didn't seem to feel duty bound to keep her informed.

In fact, Caulfield would have been impressed by such an answer. Mickey was a professional, he knew. Of course he wouldn't tell his girlfriend what secret assignment he was on!

But there were other things to consider.

One was the collection of Press Cuttings. Melia had made the news on a number of occasions, and it was never when things went right. Unlike himself, Richard thought to himself, lost in admiration for his recent successes, Melia always seemed to gain attention when things went wrong, and there were many of them.

But there was something worse.

"You've consorted with a known terrorist," Caulfield put to her.

He picked a photo from the many laid out before him and pushed it over.

24

Melia gasped. It was a picture of Emil Gorange.

Hardly someone to 'consort' with, she stuttered! He was an assassin, a hired hand, a paid killer. He put out his skills to the highest bidder, and had been richly rewarded for destroying people and property all over Europe.

Caulfield coughed and leaned forward, sensing Melia's unease. He closed in for the kill.

"You had an affair with this monster ten years ago," he alleged, "at a time when you were training in Beirut."

Melia felt her blood run cold.

How could he - How did anyone -

What the hell had happened, she wondered, that a single person in British Security had ever found out about THAT?

* * * * *

Captain Gibson faced his estranged son.

Strangely, the boy wasn't dismayed at seeing the old man, when he pulled open the ratty door to the dirty flat. He actually smiled, then moved aside to let his long-lost father walk in. Gibson tried to stifle a gasp. The air was rancid.

"How did you find me?" the kid asked.

The boss of TEEF smiled inwardly. He was a spy, wasn't he?

Once he set his mind to it, the Captain was able to delve into all the records that the United Kingdom had to offer. He was able to track the lad from the day he left school, through every part-time, short-time and low-level job he ever held, through all the signing-ons and the signing-offs, the claims for Benefit, the frauds and the lies.

At last, getting up to date, there was an address. Why not? The scrounger couldn't be receiving Benefits unless he had a front door and a letter box to send mail through. Even if the place was the worst shit-hole on the worst and most deprived estate in Greater Manchester, it was a kind of 'home' - even if it was a squat.

Because it was. Gibson Junior had broken the lock some months before, moved himself and his pregnant girlfriend in, then forced the owners - a well-known local Housing Association - to accept his claim for habitation. They weren't happy; they were working on offering the two-bedroomed accommodation to a needy couple. They weren't impressed that the trespassers had jumped the queue. Still, rules were rules. The young man was in. They had no choice.

Gibson Senior, ever the professional, sent his trusty assistant Terry into the locale to sniff out any gossip about the young man. He thought Terry the technician - with his long hair, bad clothes and geeky glasses - would be less noticeable than the ramrod straight ex-Army man, with his short haircut and well-made clothes.

He was right. The residents, when accosted by a young man in their pubs and clubs who said he was looking for a 'friend' were happy to offer help and directions. Yes, he lived in the flats. They all knew him.

"He goes by a range of names," Terry informed his boss.

He was 'Johnny G,', or 'Johnny Guitar' or 'Jackie Gibson'. It was all about his skill with the instrument. He was often seen in the pubs, it seemed, playing and singing. He was a good entertainer, they all agreed.

Not such a good provider, though. His girlfriend, the one he moved in with, moved out, when he couldn't provide enough cash for important things, like food. She didn't appreciate him prioritising guitar strings over meals.

"I'd offer you a cup of tea, but - " the kid said.

The Captain was looking around. None of the furniture looked healthy enough to sit on. He couldn't imagine what the tea cups and mugs would look like. No, that was all right. He'd forego the chance to catch something.

The room was lit by a single bulb in a wind-up lamp on a side table. The curtains were pulled, even though it was the middle of the day, and the room was gloomy and miserable. Gibson felt sorry for his son, momentarily.

Then he thought about all the chances he had given his adopted son, and how it had all been thrown back in his face.

"You obviously want something," the kid said, enjoying provoking his erstwhile parent.

What could he say? Gibson had come to say goodbye. Is that what the ne'er-do-well wanted to hear?

"Listen, Dad," the son said, wasting no time. "I need money."

Gibson didn't doubt it. Maybe money to buy some milk for the tea he would have offered if he had any teabags.

Or a kettle.

Or electricity enough for the heating of the water.

"It's not for me," the boy said.

The Captain paused. Really? well, that was a surprise. If true, it was the first selfless thing he'd ever heard the kid say.

"It's for my daughter."

Gibson looked around again. The whole place was a mess, but there was no sign of toys, or prams, or kiddies' things at all. And anyway - the girlfriend had left. There would be no baby.

No, he was told. The daughter was seven, and from a previous relationship.

Where was the wastrel mother?

"She died."

Gibson looked grim. He wasn't impressed to hear the girl's mother had expired from an accidental overdose.

Still, the fact that his son was caring for a child of his own - Well, that was impressive.

"She's got cancer."

The older man felt himself stagger. He was suddenly unsure and unsteady on his feet. Despite his best intentions, he let himself fall onto one of the overstuffed chairs. He tried to ignore the rips and stains. There were more important things to worry about now. Another life - drawing to an abrupt and unwarranted end?

"Listen, David," he said, taking a ragged breath, "I fully intend to sell the London house and put together a legacy. You can have it. You can have it all. You don't need to lie to me anymore. You don't have to create any more sob stories and fabricated crises. Just give me some time and I'll put it all in a bank account in your name - "

"It's not for me," he said again. "She needs treatment. I thought you might want to help with that."

"I've told you, one day you will be a rich man - "

"She's your grand-daughter."

Gibson gasped. He felt tears in his eyes.

Despite the fact that it was untrue. 'David', as he and his wife had chosen to call the youngster they took in, was no relation to them. Even if he had now created life, it wasn't the Gibson genes that were in the poor, unfortunate young lady. The Captain had no responsibility, no legal need to provide for illegitimate offspring.

"You want to see her?"

Gibson was rattled. It was all happening so fast.

He had chosen to face this young man, maybe for the last time. He had rooted him out and followed the clues to track him down. It still didn't mean he liked the kid. He had never appreciated the rebellious outbursts, the anger and resentment.

He'd done all a responsible parent could have done, and still it wasn't enough.

"She's lying down," he was told. "She hasn't been right since the weekend. She gets easily tired."

The Captain considered. What would he do, if confronted by a bunch of skin and bones in a filthy bed in one of the tawdry bedrooms of this awful flat? How would he react to this - ultimate - emotional blackmail?

He put out a hand and pushed himself unsteadily to his feet.

Okay, he was thinking. While I'm still strong enough, I can take anything on. Even this.

"Lead on," he said, his voice strong and determined.

* * * * *

Later that evening, Terry the technician went out on assignment.

It's not me, he was thinking. I'm the guy who sits behind computer screens, juggling bits of code, looking for CCTV evidence. He didn't often get down and dirty. In fact, he hardly ever got his feet wet. He was up in the air, a dozen floors above the ground in the new Regional Office and he ventured down for pizza, sometimes. Nothing more.

He wouldn't have even considered going out this cold and windswept night. But for one thing -

Melia asked him to.

Terry was a shadow of a human being, mostly in love with computers and the shades they showed him. But there was a single person in the world who could move him, and that was Melia. Secretly, in his own lukewarm way, he had been in love with her from the first moment they met. He couldn't talk to her without blushing, he couldn't communicate, especially in public, but he expressed his devotion in the only way he knew how: he never told her 'No'.

That's why, as the evening gloom closed in, he found himself on the banks of the River Irwell, the high-level bridge of Manchester's orbital motorway rearing above him, the blocks of Greater Manchester's biggest shopping mall and tourist destination behind him, and, in front of him - a circus Big Top.

That's what it looked like. It was a big tent, and had the customary red and white stripes for a roof. It was held up by giant wooden poles and a mess of ropes, and lights flashed and strobed all around the venue. There were cars parked on every corner and in ever crevice, and people were filing religiously towards the warmth of the entrance.

Terry pulled his woollen hat down low over his brow.

He had made an effort to disguise himself. Not because he was well known in Snake Oil circles, but because he didn't want to be noticed. He feared his bright red hair would stand out. He worried that his usual uniform of 'message' t-shirts and frayed jeans would make him memorable, so he covered them in a long duffel coat. He worried the ironwork on his face, and the blue tattoos down his chin were unusual. He didn't want anyone to see them.

Actually, he needn't have worried. There was no 'standard' attendee of this invigorating event. The bodies flocking in were all shapes and sizes, all ages and all colours. Plus the ones with disabilities, either faint weakness in capability, or complete wheelchair or maybe stick and crutch reliance. They only had one thing in common - a desire to be healed.

The vibe in the air was clear - it was like a Revivalist meeting in the Deep South of America. There was organ music wafting high and an impressive Gospel choir. The announcements were coming thick and fast through the speakers, some inside and some outside the tent, and the mood was patently being whipped up into a frenzy.

The strange thing, for Terry, was that the man he had come to see wasn't even 'Top of the Bill'.

Melia had described in some detail the name and characteristics of the man she wanted Terry to check out, but the first guy to take the microphone and storm an opening was very black and very foreign. Then, more singing. Then, a woman. It was like an old-fashioned Variety Show, where you had a range of acts. That seemed to be the approach. Even though all the 'stars' had one thing in common - an offer to heal the sick - they did it in different ways. Some were loud, some were quiet. Some dashed backwards and forwards across the stage, some stood stock still.

The first hour passed, but it didn't drag. Terry, standing at the back, near a pillar and almost invisible, watched as a succession of the sick and infirm approached the healers. Most went away happy. There was a lot of chanting.

My Goodness, Terry was thinking, I'm seeing a lot of miracles tonight!

A man came out onto the stage, waving and whooping. He held the mike in a practised hand.

"Friends, Friends," he intoned, "I want to introduce to you a new face to our Carnival of Light. He is truly a gifted giver and a mighty presence. Please take him into your hearts and show him the love we are all so used to sharing."

There was applause. People responded to the request. They couldn't wait to give this new arrival a chance.

He was a strange figure. Tall, lanky even, and a little unsteady on his feet like his customers. He wore a smart brown suit, brown tie and shoes, recently shined. He had a mop of grey hair and blinked uncertainly into the spotlights.

"Yes, Friends," the first man was saying, still trying to be helpful. "I give you - Jermy Cermoney!"

At least, that's what it sounded like.

Terry was confused. Melia had said the name was 'Jeremy Ceremony', which was unusual enough. But the Master of Ceremonies had strangled the vowels, and it came out constricted and shortened.

No matter. The body was exactly like the picture Melia had painted, relying, as she did, on the impressions she had gained at the Church. They had told her all about 'Jeremy', she said. He attended there regularly - or had done - but if Melia wanted to see the man urgently, she could catch him at the show, down at the Irwell Centre, they said.

Melia hadn't been able to make the date and time, so she sent Terry. That's everything he knew.

Terry adjusted glasses on his nose and tried to focus.

Jermy was different.

Whereas all the previous healers had been laying on hands - pushing and pulling people, dragging them out of their wheelchairs and throwing their crutches away - Jermy simply stood in the middle and waited for people to form a line. Then he got the first in the queue to sit in the single fold-up chair next to him and ran something over them.

It was a small, metallic object. Like a rod? The size and shape of a man's electric razor. Something battery powered, obviously. It was the whole thing. His whole 'act'. Jermy didn't shout, scream, or sing. He wiped people's heads and chests with his device, talked to them quietly, helped them to their feet and sent them on their way.

Terry stared. It took him a full five minutes to piece the info he had together.

It was an ultrasound massager.

That was it. That was all of it.

It was battery powered, yes, and you might find the devices in Beauty Salons, where they were used to help people tackle their wrinkles or patches of bad skin. They could seal pores, fight blemishes and cover lines.

Now, here and now, Jermy Cermoney was using the same thing to cure the sick.

Cure cancer.

Terry didn't know whether to laugh or cry. It couldn't be true! Could it? Was there anyone in the world who would claim that simple ultrasound was the solution to the worst diseases and afflictions that mankind was currently facing?

Well, yes, there was, and his name was Jeremy Something.

Terry found himself recoiling. I'm here to see this? he was thinking. What am I going to tell Melia? What should I report? How am I going to begin to describe what I'm seeing?

He found himself falling back against the canvas, so lost for words was he, and baffled.

Then he got a bigger surprise.

Looking forward again, he found himself scanning the line of people waiting for 'treatment'. They were old and young, tall and short - Someone stood out. A ramrod straight figure with slick black hair. A familiar face.

It was Captain Gibson.

Terry found himself gasping for air. Surely not! Why would the Boss be here? He needed healing?

Then, another surprise.

Behind the Captain, further back, there was another man, similar age. This one was more stoutly built, with wide shoulders, salt and pepper hair. He had no beard, just a little stubble, but his face was lined, drawn.

Still, he was unmistakable.

To Terry.

Of all the people who worked at Regional Office, naught but one would have any idea who this old guy was. Terry knew because he had access to all the Personnel records, even the ones that HR weren't allowed to look into. Terry needed to see those things when he was checking on family backgrounds, personal histories. He had Full Access.

Even Captain Gibson, working his way towards the stage, wouldn't know who the man was who was standing so close behind him, or how important he was, at least to one of the team. If the Captain had, he might have been ready to chat, to swap stories, about the one person they had in common, and the life that they had shared with the younger man.

After all, this was Mickey's father.

4. CHAPTER THREE: Scars of the past

Later that same night, Melia was waiting nervously in her flat for a visitor.

It was the reason she hadn't been able to go to the Faith Healing event, and been forced to ask Terry to go in her place. She felt bad about that. She knew Terry wasn't a Field Agent, either from training or from aptitude. He was far better employed behind a desk, preferably with a bank of monitors in front of him, each flashing figures and photos, captured images and messages. He could decode and decipher, and was invaluable to the Unit. As an Action Figure, he didn't have Mickey's physique or his history. Melia thought about the comparison, then dismissed it. She wasn't inclined to think about Mickey tonight. She hadn't heard from him - which wasn't unusual - and she wasn't making an effort to reach him.

The visitor - on the other hand - Well, she had jumped at the chance to see him.

Thinking about it - brooding, while she was waiting - it was a strange coincidence that the man she was expecting was someone she hadn't seen for years, and hadn't really thought about, until Caulfield raised his name.

Gorange.

Over the years, the man who called himself Emil Gorange had come in and gone out of Melia's life at regular intervals. Mostly, he had caused her trouble. There was a time, she couldn't remember when, that it seemed like he had dedicated his life to ending hers. He seemed to arrive in her orbit with the sole intention of causing her death. Luckily, he was rather bad at it and was repeatedly unsuccessful, which was strange, bearing in mind that he was a professional assassin.

There were plenty of other words to describe the jobs he did. He was a professional hit-man, a part-time terrorist, a Soldier of Fortune, a mercenary. Most of them were unpleasant epithets, but they all aimed at capturing the concentrated evil of a soul who was ending to commit murder and mayhem to order - as long as the price was right.

Melia had never had anything but contempt for the man. He hadn't shown her a trace of kindness or compassion, and she regarded him with the same mix of fear and caution that she would show to a crocodile. The croc, of course, couldn't help be anything but what he was and didn't hurt people or animals through rancour or revenge. Gorange, the record showed, was a man driven by the basest of human emotions. He was the antithesis of all the principles Melia espoused.

When the call came through - diverted via an intermediary - Melia might have been afraid. That would have been her earlier response, but her contact assured her that things had changed. Gorange had changed. He was not the man he was. He had been battered and bruised and was near submission.

The problem, Melia was told, was that he had suffered a number of assaults in recent times, and was badly injured. He had lost the use of one hand, could hardly walk, and even if he was still motivated by anger and resentment, he didn't have the means to carry things through. He was a shadow of the threat he had once been.

The doorbell rang.

Melia's flat was on the second floor. She could look out a window and see anyone standing by the main door, in a pool of light shed by the nearest street-lamp. She saw no one. He must have been hugging the shadows.

She pressed a button and heard the click of the downstairs door, then the shuffling gait of someone on the stairs. The, at last, a polite knock on her own door. She went to open it.

A stooped figure in black clothes stood to one side, bent into himself and shrunken.

Melia leapt back in alarm, not just at the shape of the caller, but the pallor of his face. Even in the dim light of the hallway, she could see the battered cheeks and the lined forehead. One eye was nearly closed.

A memory leapt into her mind. He had been the victim of an acid attack, someone in the office had told her. Someone had thrown a whole bottle of acid over his head. It had burned him badly. He was no deformed.

Melia took a deep breath, and reminded herself what she was doing.

She wasn't there for his benefit - he was there for hers. Caulfield had raised questions about her loyalty and commitment to the cause. She wanted to hear from Gorange how he felt about their previous encounters. She needed to know that her boss, the Deputy Director was wrong, and there had never been anything but animosity on Gorange's part.

Melia stood politely to one side, and let him shuffle past her, through the hall and into the living room. She followed on, thinking of offering to take his coat, but he seemed unwilling to shed any layers. She waiting.

She considered. She had thought of having a gun handy, just in case, but what was clear was that this scrapheap of a former terrorist was nothing like the opponent she had once known.

Melia formed a smile. So, in a sense, she was thinking, I have won. He is ruined. I have survived.

He waited while she fetched him a drink, then slowly, painfully, he lowered himself on to the settee.

"It was Christian terrorists," he told her. "They did this to me. Ironic, when you think about it. Their religion would surely tell them that such a thing was wrong. Perhaps they ignore their precious Good Book. Luckily, I have no religion."

His speech was raspy, but the accent was there still, vaguely Eastern European and slurred.

"Why would they want to target you?" she asked automatically, then realised the question was almost redundant.

How many people had he killed? How many of their relatives and comrades wanted him dead? It was innumerable.

"Who have I killed - recently?" Gorange said, as if really looking for an answer.

"It's your job," Melia reminded him. They shared a history - and a profession.

"One that has reached a natural end," he observed slyly.

He was still in his street clothes, scarf pulled around his neck, woollen hat keeping his badly scarred head warm.

"I'm glad you agreed to see me," he noted, and held out his glass for another drink of wine.

"You're retiring?"

"I'm dying."

Melia had jumped to that conclusion, seeing the terrible state he was in. But she was wrong about details.

"I have cancer," he told her. "These injuries - they are annoying, but not deadly. No, it's my own body that has turned against me, and is devouring itself, cell against cell. I will soon lie down and never get up again."

"Then I need you to tell me something important," Melia said urgently.

She related some of the accusations she had been faced with, when Caulfield began his 'investigation'.

"I need to hear you say," she told him, "that our interactions were never anything other than professional."

He took a deep breath. He knew their lives had intertwined. They had found themselves on opposite sides of the fight over so many battlefields. In a way, it was so obvious. What did she expect him to say?

"We clashed," he agreed, "and some times you bettered me. Sometimes you prevailed because you had so many friends and allies - that Mickey character, of course, and your formidable superior, the Captain Gibson."

He paused, as if struggling for breath. Melia wondered if he had the strength for this conversation.

"Melia," he said slowly, deliberately, "surely you realise that if I wanted you dead - then, back then when I was fit and active - it would not have been a problem, at any time. It was not luck or comrades that kept you alive."

"Then what was it?"

"Why, my dear girl, it was the fact that I was in love with you. Always. Forever. I loved you from the first moment I ever set eyes on you, and my heart has not faltered through the decade we have known each other."

Melia couldn't breathe. Something had caught in her throat and she couldn't get a word out.

He raised his head and his gaze settled on her. Despite the ravaged face and the changes he had undergone, the look was clear and unmistakeable. It confirmed everything he had put into words. His heart was on his sleeve.

"I don't know what to say," she managed at last, forcing the words out.

He continued looking at her, as if enjoying every moment they were together, as if determined to make the very, very most of the short time he had left. Every second counted.

Neither of them moved, for a long time further.

*   *   *   *   *

The very next day, as soon as was decent, Caulfield got dressed up and went into Manchester.

He was rarely seen in the big city, even he had to admit, but he was a man on a mission. From that day he'd been on the bus, feeling sorry for himself, a thought had been building and growing in his head. It wasn't his fault!

None of it. None of the bad things that had happened in his life.

Where did he ever get the idea he was to blame? Maybe because that was what his elders and betters had led him to believe, ever since he was a nipper. Well, that was like brainwashing, wasn't it? he thought to himself. You tell a kid something often enough, and they start to accept it. 'Not good enough' maybe, or 'You're never going to amount to anything'. That was the sort of programming that could destroy anyone's confidence.

But more than that. The others - those people who hadn't been ground down, excluded and put upon - they had proceeded through life with heads held high and an inexhaustible feeling of entitlement. That was something Richard Caulfield had never had. On the contrary, his belief system was that life was hard and he would be forced to fight for every crumb he could ever sweep up from the Top Table. It wasn't for him, that place. He would never be allowed in.

He would confront them, he decided. None of us are getting any younger. If I ever do want to progress, to get beyond 'Deputy' anything, he said to himself, then I will have to break through the glass ceiling, in order to progress.

Caulfield arrived in the city centre and walked across Albert Square, outside Manchester Town Hall. It was an impressive edifice, but it seemed strangely quiet and dark. Then he saw the notice. 'Closed for Refurbishment' it said, and under that: 'See you in 2024'. He chuckled. If we all live that long, he was thinking. It wasn't certain.

There were cafes on all sides of the Square, but most seemed closed at this early hour. He wandered down John Dalton Street and found an old-fashioned, greasy kind of place. They were serving fried food - bacon, eggs, sausage, black pudding. All fried, all greasy. I haven't been in a place like this since - He couldn't remember when.

We are all so 'Health Conscious', he was thinking. We avoid fat, frying, lumps of meat. Not today, he decided.

It was strangely satisfying. All of it. Not just the food, but sitting by a window and watching all the busy boys and girls hurrying to their early starts. Not me, he was thinking. I set my own course. I am my own slave driver, no one else.

It wasn't true, of course. He took orders directly from Captain Gibson, and he'd better be quick about it. No, he had never argued with The Old Man. Actually, he respected the old soldier. Gibson had principles, he knew, but he also had Common Sense and a good sense of strategy. If Gibson said it was a good idea, well, it probably was.

But something had changed. From deep inside Caulfield, the recent resentment about being passed over for the top job, had brought out a teenage streak of rebellion and contrariness. I will not accept orders unquestioned, he decided. Not any more. I am not a robot, I am a human being. They cannot treat me this way, he was repeating to himself.

Of course, an outside observer might have seen something different. Richard Caulfield, the man who had always been lazy and hard to get started, appeared to have simply slowed entirely and ground to a halt. That was his 'rebellion'. He had simply switched off, moving from low gear into no gear.

How long before he actually went into reverse?

There were free newspapers on a shelf. After eating himself to a standstill, Caulfield ordered more coffee and started reading a paper. Time passed, while the Deputy Director perused the tragedies of the day. Nothing moved him.

At last, maybe an hour later, he reluctantly put away the reading matter, pushed plates and cups to one side, shook himself, clambered to his feet, dusted himself down, and walked out into the grey morning. It was Manchester, he was thinking. It was either raining, or about to rain, that was what they said about the city. It was unusually true.

He walked back up the road, then along, then down and found himself on a parallel street down to the river. It's somewhere around here, he was thinking. That's what he had been told. He wasn't sure of precise details.

He walked past the building at first. Why not? It was designed to be a secret.

Caulfield was looking for the Regional Headquarters of The Sacred Society. It was a nondescript frontage in a row of Victorian offices and the occasional shop. There was a small, discreet brass plaque near the door. 'Manchester', it said.

He pressed the bell and stood back. Someone would be in, he reasoned. Didn't people live on the premises?

A small, round, black woman poked her head out of the door, and looked him up and down.

Caulfield gaped, his prejudices shaken. Wasn't this meant to be the bastion of the white middle-class?

Then his suspicions were confirmed. She introduced herself. She was the cleaner. Yes, she made an early start.

He was surprised that she pulled the door further open and ushered him in, then went to fetch help.

Caulfield looked around. The hall was ornate. He was facing a marble staircase. There were chandeliers. It screamed money. There had been investment in this place. It was not just historic, but well funded too.

A young man in a plaid jumper and slacks came out from behind the stairs. He was smiling.

He took Caulfield's hand. He shook it, but in a strange way. Ah, Caulfield was thinking. The secret shake.

"How can I help you?" the youngster said. He had a steady gaze and was inspecting the visitor with a quizzical eye.

"I'd like to talk to somebody," Caulfield said.

"You want to join?"

Richard Caulfield gasped. He felt a catch in his throat. There was almost a tear in his eye, suddenly.

"I've never been allowed to join," he confided to the confident young man.

"Nonsense," was his reply. "Things have changed. We are much more open now. Don't worry."

The young man looked around, as if making up his mind where to start. Maybe a little tour of the building?

The kid said: "We like to get to know people, of course, before ever issuing an invitation. Let me show you the rooms, maybe some of the paraphernalia. There is something of a museum on the second floor. Then we can sit down and talk about Responsibilities. You seem a reasonable kind of person. I'm sure there is nothing you wouldn't understand."

He had clearly taken in Caulfield's smart suit, his debonair manner and his air of affluence. Things seemed to be going well, and nothing had even been asked. But the opposite was true too: Yes, Caulfield had been turned down for the Society, both in Hong Kong and when he lived in London. It had hurt him, and sparked his negativity.

Could he ever get over that? Caulfield made up his mind in a heartbeat. If they let me in, he was thinking, I will be their sternest defender and their most ardent supporter. Everything I've thought before - forget it!

The young man steered his caller towards the stairs. The cleaner was nowhere to be seen.

As they climbed, Caulfield's gaze drifted to the portraits that lined the walls. There was the Queen, of course, and several Dukes, but a familiar figure suddenly caught his eye, standing outside a country pub, beside a horse.

It was the current Home Secretary, member of the Cabinet in the government of Great Britain.

* * * * *

Later that same day, nearer lunch time, Jermy Cermoney was walking down the road to St Cyprian's church.

Jeremy was feeling confident. The healing 'circus' of the night before had gone surprisingly well for him. Most of the people who sat for his treatment stated that they felt 'better' and some were even willing to agree with him that they were 'cured'. Those, the satisfied ones, he had immediately ushered to one side and forced to fill in comments on his web page. They seemed happy to add their Testimonials to the ones already there. It was a growing wave of opinion in his favour, Jeremy was thinking. I am building my reputation and faith in my methods.

The rucksack on his back felt warm and comforting. It contained a number of ultrasound devices. He was testing some of them. They were newly obtained from China and were rated at a range of outputs. He didn't know whether the 8mHz was the optimum for the sorts of results he wanted. He planned to see if the smaller ones were just as effective.

Not that that he would necessarily be welcome at the church, he knew.

Technically speaking, he had been banned from the premises. But that was only for being a little too enthusiastic with his offer of 'cures'. He shouldn't have pressured people, especially the homeless ones. Some of them were a little nervous, sensitive, suspicious, and apt to complain. He would have to be more cautious about who he approached.

But today was a good day. The church had a Starvation Lunch on this day, every week. It attracted a good crowd. For some, it was the chance of a free feed. For others, the simple soup, bread and cheese was meant to be a reminder of how many people in the world couldn't rely on a 'square meal' every day. They ate the meagre food thoughtfully, then went into the body of the church for some prayers with the Vicar. It was a spiritually uplifting experience.

For Jeremy, it was an audience. It was hard for him to get people in the same place that he could badger and bully. Sitting around the tables, mainly thinking about eating, they were an easy target for a super salesman.

"Jeremy, isn't it?" a voice behind him said.

Jeremy turned around. A young man, smartly dressed, carrying a briefcase, had hurried up.

"I don't think - "

"I'm Martin Muffin," the man said.

Jeremy gaped. This was - This man was his hero! The Muffin Institute had pioneered the use of ultrasound.

"We've never met," Jeremy noted, extending a hand, "but this is a real pleasure!"

"What happened to your face?"

They were standing in the road. On both sides were new houses, provided by a property developer, with the assistance and support of Salford City Council. Straight ahead was the church, with its trim garden out front and its ornate gates.

It was a ludicrous place to stop and stand and have any sort of discussion, but Jeremy was nervous about taking the man into the church - especially if the Minister was still negative and antagonistic about his work.

No, the weather was fine, if a little cold. They could stop here for a minute or two, for a chat.

Jeremy said, informatively: "I had a motor accident about ten years ago. I was badly damaged and lost about thirty per cent of my brain. I was laid in bed for five months, and then had to learn to walk and talk, all over again."

Mr Muffin seemed to consider that for a while. He nodded slowly, as if weighing every word.

"And when," he asked quietly, "did you become convinced of the efficacy of ultrasound in curing cancer?"

"I was badly hurt, but I never stopped thinking," Jeremy assured him. "When I saw your articles on the internet, I decided to buy my own device and conduct my own experiments. They turned out better than I'd hoped."

"You say, 'MY' articles ? Which ones are you thinking about?"

"The Institute did research on ultrasound, even as far back as the '80s."

"That was my father," Martin said sharply. "However, he never, ever, EVER, said anything about a cure."

"Oh, I'm sure I read it - "

"He demonstrated that ultrasound could be used to find tumours," Mr Muffin said, directly contradicting everything that Jeremy was asserting. "Just as, in the same way, midwives can used ultrasound as a non-invasive way of viewing a foetus in utero, he showed that similar ultrasound devices would illuminate cancerous growths in the body. In CERTAIN cases, not all. Cancers are different and show up in different ways. It's not possible to use them in every case."

"He showed that ultrasound devices could reduce the size of tumours - "

"In CERTAIN cases," Martin agreed, "and in a small way. He didn't say - at any point - that ultrasound, in itself, could cure cancer, and absolutely not ALL cancers. Why, he only looked at a tiny sample - "

"I have had outstanding results."

Martin Muffin took a deep breath. He seemed to be fighting to control his temper. He was trying to sound reasonable.

"You have stolen my firm's research," he said, seething. "You have misrepresented our results. You have used my name, and attested conclusions and propositions to us that we have never made - "

"What do you want me to do?"

Martin looked the older man up and down. He noted the ravaged face, the slight stoop, the unsteady stance. He almost felt sorry for the guy, with his car accident and his uncomfortable life.

He hated having to take away what was probably the main thing keeping him going right now.

"You need to desist," he assured Jeremy. "Stop. Stop using my name and the name of my Institute. Stop mentioning us in any publications, or any notes, blogs, or videos that you do on the internet."

"I have a device in my bag right now - "

"It's a toy! It's a handheld model that they use in Beauty Salons. It can't possibly do what you claim it can do!"

Jeremy was silent for a while. He seemed to be thinking. At length, he spoke and was surprisingly calm.

"You want me to stop?" he said. "So far, all I can hear are threats. You've heard of 'The Carrot and the Stick'. You've produced the stick. I want to know what else you've got."

"I really don't see - " Mr Muffin began.

"Offer me a carrot," Jeremy suggested.

5. ## CHAPTER FOUR: Always the hero

Later that afternoon, Terry kept an appointment with Mickey's Dad.

Strictly speaking, he ambushed the old man.

Terry was the computer guy at TEEF, the geek who could make the machines talk. It wasn't that difficult for him to scan the hotels in the city centre and find out where his quarry was staying. He even called up CCTV images from the cameras outside in the street and caught sight of Mickey's Dad going in. Then, a switch to internal cameras, and Terry could place him in the bar. Good. It was The Trade Hotel, a landmark on Peter Street. Easy to find.

There was one more thing. Terry was good with his hands and a soldering iron. He had made a little incentive.

Mickey's Dad liked a drink, that was clear, but he was also more than a little discreet. He wasn't sitting in a window seat, or one of the couches near the entrance. He had found himself a quiet corner where he could keep an eye on the door, but wouldn't be noticed by people moving in or out. Ah, training, Terry was thinking. A clear sign of an experienced spy.

Terry took a deep breath and did something he didn't normally do: he became an extrovert.

"Excuse me," he said boldly, approaching his target. "You were at the Big Top last night, weren't you?"

Mickey's Dad gave made a good attempt at acting non-committal.

"Why would that interest you?" he said, not overtly antagonistic at this stage.

"I have something you might be interested in," Terry said, swinging his briefcase onto the low table.

"So? You want to sell me something," Mickey's Dad said, visibly relaxing.

Clearly, he didn't see a salesman as a threat.

Good, Terry was thinking. My plan is working well, so far.

He nodded and smiled at the older man, trying to win his confidence and play to the story he had worked out.

"You buy me a drink," he suggested grandly, "and I'll show you something you won't be able to refuse."

Mickey's Dad seemed amused at the effort the so-called 'Sales' person was putting in. He played along.

There were waiters in the room and the older man called one over. Terry made sure to order something expensive.

"You're going to make me pay?" Mickey's Dad said, as if he had expected it.

"What price would you put on your life?" Terry asked, knowing that's what a bad salesperson would say.

Then he kept his 'customer' waiting, building the suspense. He tried a little small talk until the drinks arrived - Mickey's Dad took a top-up, not letting the 'round' pass him by - and Terry sipped the cocktail he had ordered appreciatively.

"They make them better here than in Ibiza," he said, as if he was young and used to holidaying in the sun.

Mickey's Dad was looking down on him now. He didn't think he would be troubled by the offer, whatever it was.

"I saw you in the queue," Terry said at last. "I guess you were impressed with Mr Cermoney's set-up. But let me ask you this - wouldn't you be better off with your own private machine, at home? Wouldn't you like to OWN the cure?"

Mickey's Dad nodded, sipped his drink, and waited for his new-found friend to go through his sales patter. He had no suspicions. Why would he? He had never met Terry, and didn't know he happened to work beside Mickey, his son.

Terry prised open his base with a flourish. Inside was a small, hand-held ultrasound device, complete with its own charging lead, brushes, cleaner fluid and lubricator. It was neatly arranged, tightly packed.

"Look at the finish on this case," Terry enthused. "See the arrangement. There's a book to go with it, but you don't need complicated instructions. You saw one like this at work, during the show, and now you could do it yourself."

"How much would it set me back?"

Terry ignored the question, as he knew a salesman would.

"You're going to need a series of treatments," he said. "You could book in with Jermy at his Clinic, and end up paying an arm and a leg. I can let you have this - the whole kit - at a knock-down price. Special Offer, today only."

Mickey's Dad put out a hand and ran his hand over the device at the centre of the case.

"Take it out. Try it," Terry said. "Where is your problem area, can I ask?"

"My throat," the older man said, lifted the ultrasound and ran it around his neck.

The hand-held device was charged up. When Mickey's Dad hit the switch, it buzzed, as it should.

Terry said: "This little collection, the whole caboodle, will retail at four fifty in the shops. But, I can help you with that. Like I said, I'm prepared to make it worth your while. Today - a third off."

"Half," Mickey's Dad said.

Terry paused, as if considering the haggling. He needed more interaction, he knew.

"You want to live, don't you?" he said, a little provocatively. He hoped he wasn't overdoing it.

"I've had a long life," the old man said. "I'm not sure I need to prolong it."

That couldn't be true, Terry reasoned. He had been there for the Healing, after all.

"Maybe not for yourself," Terry said, pushing it. "But what about your family?"

"I have no family. I had a wife. I had two children, a son and a daughter. But they're all dead."

Terry fought hard not to react.

He tried to watch idly as Mickey's Dad played the device across his chest, then up either side of his neck.

Why would he lie? Terry was wondering.

Firstly, he admitted to a son, but then asserted he was 'dead'. Mickey's not dead!

Then he mentioned a daughter. Mickey doesn't have a sister!

Mickey's Dad, relaxed, enjoying the bargaining, suddenly changed.

He was looking off across the room, towards the bar. It was if he recognised someone. A face? A problem?

He abruptly put down the pieces, finished his drink and stood up.

"I have to go now," he said. "Give me your card and I'll find you on the internet."

Terry had taken the precaution of preparing just such a contact card. He handed one over. Mickey's Dad didn't even pause to shake hands. He moved around the table and headed for the door.

Terry jumped up, determined to follow him. He had so many unanswered questions!

"I couldn't help overhearing," a voice said, to his side.

Terry turned. An old man with a straggly beard was leaning out of his easy chair. He stood up.

"I'd like to have a gander at your kit," he said, moving across.

"Take it. Take it!" Terry muttered, and hurried away.

Terry was assuming that Mickey's Dad was staying in the hotel, and, if he left the bar, the obvious thing for him to do would be to head for his room upstairs. But he didn't do that. The old man walked straight past the stairs, avoided the lifts, and walked through the glass atrium at the back of the hotel towards the entrance at the rear.

Terry saw him going into the street, then heading left.

Mickey's Dad wasn't hurrying, just walking determinedly and steadily. Terry was able to keep up.

He saw Mickey's Dad go down to Peter Street and turn right. Terry trailed along. His quarry was moving towards The Great North Western, another big hotel, facing St Peter's Square.

Terry saw him bound up the steps at the front and disappear into the massive foyer.

He was staying there? Did he go to The Trade Hotel for a drink, simply to avoid being seen? Was he afraid he was being watched, or followed? He was on his guard, then, but why? Who did he have to fear? Who would want to hurt him?

Terry paused. If Mickey's Dad was staying at The North Western, he couldn't simply bound into Reception. It would be too obvious. Terry looked around. I'll go round the back, maybe try and sneak in the Staff Entrance, he decided.

He walked swiftly up the street at the side and was just in time to see Mickey's Dad come OUT of the Staff Entrance. He crossed the road and kept going, in the direction of The Bridgewater Concert Hall.

Terry was staggered. So much trouble! So, it looked like Mickey's Dad wasn't actually staying at either hotel, and was using all his wiles now to evade pursuit. He had booked in at The Trade Hotel though, Terry knew that from the records. Well, that was an expensive bluff, to book a room, then not use it.

It was all a bit more than he had anticipated, Terry was thinking. He had guessed that the Dad was in town to see Mickey. Maybe not. He had thought the old man was genuinely sick and had been to see Jermy Cermoney to get well. Maybe not. He had talked about retirement, leaving his previous employment behind him. Maybe not.

Terry clenched his jaw and made himself a little promise. I'm going to get to the bottom of this little mystery, he decided. For all our sakes. For me. For Mickey. For Melia. For all of us.

He crossed the road, hot in pursuit.

* * * *

It was a good job that Terry left The Trade Hotel when he did. If he'd stayed, he would have bumped into Melia.

She came in the entrance off Peter Street and headed straight for the bar. She was a few minutes early for her appointment, and decided that gave her time for a drink and a chance to catch her breath.

The waiter, a young man, eager to impress, spotted the elegant young lad and hurried over.

"Australian," Melia told him. White. Fizzy. She liked her wine the same way she liked her men.

The man made a great show of noting the order in his small black book.

"What's the fuss?" Melia asked him, ready for a few brief words of conversation.

The kid looked behind him.

Oh, yes. A man with red hair had brought in some kind of medical contraption and had been showing it to a client. All the people in the bar had noticed. Some of the older people wanted a go of it.

"People!" Melia chuckled, unaware of what the fuss was all about. She felt indulgent. Let them make a fuss, she thought.

She chose a seat near the window, not to see anyone, or watch the street, but just to feel as though she was still in touch, still part of the world. She had come to the hotel to meet a friend, and she was conscious that her 'friendship' with the man was cutting her off from her own friends and colleagues. He was a man who divided opinion.

He was Gorange.

Melia received the wine gratefully and gulped it down. She needed a drink, she realised, to calm her nerves.

Goodness knows why I agreed to meet him again, she was thinking. I mean, we have history, sure, but most of it hasn't been pleasant. He tried to kill me, she recalled, then paused. She wondered if she'd have to rewrite her memories. He had said, after all, that he hadn't tried that hard - because he was in love with her.

It made no sense. It didn't make her feel flattered, or in the least bit joyful. Why, he was one of the top assassins in the world. Being his target was something of a privilege. Being his infatuations was - what? An embarrassment?

Melia finished her drink and made a beeline for Reception. She didn't need to - he had told her his room number - but she had a strange urge to check, to verify the information he was feeding her. She still didn't trust him.

Yes, he was on the fourth floor.

"I want ot surprise him," she said to the clerk with a wink, intimating some kind of personal liaison.

The man behind the desk smiled ruefully, and busied himself on other matters.

Melia climbed the stairs. If I was him, she was thinking, I would have tipped the clerk and told him to phone me if I had any callers. It was a test, Melia was thinking. If I knock on his door and he knows I'm in the building, then yes, he has taken precautions. Not just against her, of course. He had plenty of other enemies, those that were still alive.

Melia emerged from the staircase on the right floor. She wasn't even breathless. Who needs a gym? she thought with delight. I'm fit, and I can keep fit by little bits of regular exercise.

She heard someone knocking. Looking up, she saw a figure outside a door at the far end of the corridor, just about where Gorange's room would be. As she strolled towards the man, she saw the door open, and all that happened next.

The visitor reached in and grabbed the person he had come to see. He heaved him out, and flung him past him, right into the wall opposite. There was the loud clunk of a body hitting something solid.

"Hi!" Melia shouted, and started to run.

The attacker saw her coming and seemed to decide to abandon his assault immediately. He ran off towards the stairs at the far end of the corridor, flung open the door and vanished into the stairwell.

Melia arrived and helped the victim to his feet. He was shaken, a little shocked, but not really injured.

It wasn't Gorange.

There was a person standing in the open doorway of the next room. Now that, THAT was Gorange.

He was staring at Melia. He seemed slightly amused. He watched her play First Aider.

Melia helped the upset man back into his room, then followed Gorange into his own. She was pleased he had a bottle of wine on ice. He graciously poured some into a fluted glass and handed it to her.

"My Angel of Mercy," he said mockingly.

"I thought it was you."

"It should have been me," Gorange said, smiling.

He had booked that room, he said, knowing it was a good one. Then he had knocked on this door and given the man a story about him being 'upgraded'. The occupant was happy to move his bags next door, and let the man with a burned face have the inferior room. He didn't seem inclined to question his supposed good luck.

"You could have killed him!" Melia admonished.

"No, see what happened," Gorange said calmly.

It was true. The caller hadn't intended to kill the person in that room, merely scare him maybe, or give him some message that he was being watched. He had pulled him about, flung him across the carpet. Perhaps he intended a punch or two, and then he would have left, anyway, Gorange asserted,

Melia made a sour face. You're good at this life, she told him.

"No," he said firmly, "I'm not. Not any more. I've lost my edge. It puts me at risk. I'm in more danger than ever. Punks like that will seek me out, and I won't be able to resist them one day. One of them will get me, eventually."

He sat on the edge of the dressing table. It wasn't a large room and there was only one chair.

"I'm sick of all the killing," he told her, repeating his message. "That's why I invented the 'Rucksack' campaign. I was trying to say to people, 'You don't need the blood, the carnage. You can still intimidate people, even without real bombs. Just plant a few bags and cause some disruption.' They weren't willing to listen. They want to hear the bang."

If Caulfield had been there, he would have asked: "You? You started the 'Rucksacks'?" But Melia wasn't aware of what was playing out. She hadn't been asked to be involved. It wasn't her investigation.

Her life was on a different track. She had been put forward by Captain Gibson for promotion, which was why her private life was being gone over with a fine comb, and turning over the Gorange rock had meant he had re-appeared in her life. Now what am I going to do? she wondered. What am I going to say to him? What have I decided?

She really didn't know what to think.

Melia had lost her nemesis and gained a Gentleman admirer. What was she going to do with him?

* * * * *

As for rucksacks, at that precise moment Caulfield was having his own problems with a live one.

I never should have swapped to trams, he was thinking, looking at the crowd milling around him.

Why not? It had been a logical thought. Greater Manchester was an area that benefited not just from a comprehensive bus service, but also a network of suburban trains - and, since the 1990s - a collection of modern trams.

The Deputy Director had got bored with watching people get on and off buses, and was looking for a change of scene. Forget the wheels, he was thinking, I'll get on to the tracks. Trams, it is then, for starters.

The obvious prime choice - thinking like a terrorist - was the tram line from Piccadilly Station in the centre of Manchester out to Eccles. Mainly, because it happened to pass through the area of Salford Quays, which was where the BBC were now based, as well as other TV stations, support companies and media groups. A 'high profile' target, as the Security Services might say. If a bomb went off in television land, then it would get on to the television news, wouldn't it? And that's what the terror people wanted above all - publicity.

It was an interesting tram line. As the trams went through the old docklands, they twisted and turned, went up and down and all around. Caulfield couldn't see exactly why. It wasn't as though the buildings they skirted around were very important. It was almost as though the designers had been inspired to make the passage 'interesting', by adding a few overpasses. It added to the time it took, Caulfield was thinking sullenly, as they came back out of the Quays and headed for the river, making their predictable track back towards the city.

That's when something unpredictable happened.

The tram had just left Exchange Quay station, turned left and was beginning the climb up towards the bridge that crossed the River Irwell. Caulfield was marvelling at the incline. Why, trams seemed to be able to go up hills that would stop a normal train. Not the tram! It ground along the rails and hauled itself high into the air.

As it did so, there was the noise of something sliding along the floor. The Deputy Director looked down.

It was a rucksack.

Right, there had been a rucksack under one of the seats, and the change in angle of the floor had caused it to slide backwards. That wasn't a disaster, but what was strange - and worrying - was that no one reached down to grab it. After all, if it had belonged to someone - anyone - they would want to retrieve it, right?

No one did.

Caulfield kept his eye on the bag. The tram trundled across the river bridge, then turned extreme left and pulled into Pomona Station. Caulfield leapt to his feet, hurtled along and banged on the driver's door.

"Code 21!" he boomed.

The driver looked round, startled, but he'd heard the message. He pulled his key out of the lock, powered down the tram, left his seat and evacuated the vehicle.

"Everybody out!" Caulfield shouted, to left and right. "Assemble in orderly fashion on the platform."

There was some grumbling. A journey interrupted, a deadline missed. It's for your own good, Caulfield wanted to tell them, but of course that wasn't true. It was a rucksack. It was a demonstration of trouble by 'The Rucksack Raiders', no doubt, a fake 'bomb', an irritation and a nuisance, but their lives weren't really at risk.

No, the real reason the Deputy Director had to clear the carriage was to get them out of the scene, so that the Forensics Team would have the best chance of gathering evidence, without interference.

A man said: "I have an urgent appointment in Manchester."

Caulfield looked him up and down, giving him the benefit of his most contemptuous look.

"I've phoned in," the driver said. "They're backing a tram down from Cornbrook Station, the next stop. It's only about three hundred yards. They'll pull in at the platform end, and you can board the other vehicle to continue your journey."

"So," the Deputy Director told the complainant, "a minimal delay."

"Can I go back in?" a girl said.

Caulfield stared. What had she said? Were all these people crazy?

"There's evidence at the back of the unit," he told her falteringly, struggling to explain politely. "I can't have you contaminating the Crime Scene. I hope you understand."

"I'm a student," the young person said. "I left my bag behind. You shouted, I was confused. It's got all my notes in, my laptop, my phone and my draft Dissertation. I can't go home without them."

They were standing at the front of the tram. The girl pointed in through the window. There was a blue and black bag on a seat. They could all see it clearly. It was a rucksack!

"That's yours?" Caulfield asked her. "That's definitely yours? You can confirm you own it?"

"It's at the front," she pointed out. "I can dodge in without disturbing your other bag, the one at the back."

There was mumbling from the other passengers. They all seemed to approve of the young lady's request, its reasonableness. Caulfield saw that he couldn't refuse without provoking an insurrection.

It took less than a minute for the driver to open the nearest door with his special key, the girl to go inside and return with her bag. She was smiling, delighted. All the bystanders seemed pleased too. Everyone was happy.

"It's only a dummy, the other bag," Caulfield said softly, grumbling to the driver, who he thought might be on his side.

"I saw it," the girl said. "There are wires poking out of the top."

"It's a fake," the Deputy Director reassured her.

"It's ticking."

Five minutes later, Caulfield was standing back in the tram, looking down at the offending rucksack.

He was on the phone.

"It has a label on the side," he reported to the Bomb Squad. It read, 'Rucksack Rebels'. "It's not The Rucksack Raiders. Maybe it's a different group. What do you think?"

"We're not going to get there in time," the Sergeant told him. "You need to grab it and heft it into the river. Don't make a fuss, just do it. You can't take the chance and wait. It's not an option."

Caulfield looked around. Pomona Station was built up on pillars, so that it was level with the bridge. It was ten metres up in the air. Behind him, the tram door was open and beyond the platform fence there was open air and an abrupt drop. He took a deep breath. He was thinking, I can do this. I am here. No one else is. I need to act.

The Deputy Director lifted the bag, as ordered, spun on his heel, took five steps out of the tram and onto the edge and threw the rucksack out over the water. It blew up a few seconds later, when it was just short of the river.

There was applause.

Caulfield looked up and was pleased to see the dozens of grateful passengers were giving him a standing ovation.

A hero, he was thinking. I am a hero today.

Again.

6. CHAPTER FIVE: Fakes

A few days later, Mickey's Dad was sitting on a trolley in Salford's main hospital.

It was embarrassing. He was wearing nothing but a hospital gown, and that was done up the back, badly. He could feel breezes around his rear, but he didn't want to turn and stare. He was keeping his eyes up, refusing to look around.

He consoled himself with one thought. Even though he had been waiting an hour, it was nothing like a record for this place. They seemed to make a habit of dawdling. He had been talking to a guy in the Waiting Room earlier.

"They have to see us within two hours. It's a rule," the man assured him.

So, Dad was pleased when someone arrived and they took him in to a cubicle. He thought it meant he was on his way.

Instead, they merely took his clothes away and told him to put the nightshirt on. Then, there was squawking outside and he was told he would have to wait in the corridor while they dealt with an 'Emergency'. Fair enough, he was thinking. But wait, this wasn't the Emergency department! Why were they having urgent problems there? People came in for treatment. They were regulars. Nothing should be going wrong. There shouldn't be problems. There shouldn't.

After what seemed like an age - and Mickey's Dad couldn't know the time taken, since they had removed his watch from him - a porter appeared and wheeled him back into the screened-off area. A curtain was pulled round and a man in a white coat came in.

"I'm Dr Porter, your anaesthetist. I'm going to give you a muscle relaxant," he said cheerfully.

Mickey's Dad leaned back on the plumped up pillow. A needle? He wasn't expecting that.

He was expecting a simple check-up, to see how his illness was progressing. Because it was getting worse, he knew that. The initial x-rays had shown a growing tumour in his stomach. It wasn't going away. He'd refused radical surgery, and turned down radiology. They'd been giving him some medicine, but it was mostly hormonal. He wasn't having chemo.

They told me I might die, Mickey's Dad was thinking. Well, that wouldn't be so bad.

People have been trying to kill me for years. I'm used to living with the prospect of it all coming to an end.

I can live with that, he was thinking dreamily. I've lived with death and I can negotiate my own.

Someone else came into the area, and Mickey's Dad realised he had been drifting off. Where had the other guy gone, the one with the injections? This new man was busying himself at the monitors.

"My name is Dr Muffin," he said, over his shoulder. "I am Martin Muffin from The Muffin Institute. Your consultant has allowed me access to your records, in the interests of a Study we are doing into aggressive forms of cancer."

Go ahead, Mickey's Dad was thinking. Whatever you want - look, study, gather information.

The man was chatty. "We have pioneered the use of ultrasound in identifying and keeping tabs on tumours. I know you've had x-rays but this is a non-invasive and far more accurate method. Would you mind if I ran a device over your

JC's Cure for Cancer

chest and down to your stomach? I will have to apply a lubricant first. It will feel oily and cold."

The older man waved him on. Do it, Doc, he said. Anything for the advancement of science!

In truth, Mickey's Dad felt out of it, drifting in and out of dreamland. Whatever the first guy gave me, it was powerful stuff, he was thinking. He felt woozy, not at all alert. He couldn't care what happened next.

"Right, I'm getting good results on the screen," the visiting doctor was saying. "You want to see?"

Not really, Mickey's Dad was thinking. Who wants to view the thing that's killing them?

You watch it, Doc. Watch it and rub it out, that would be better. Get rid of it, maybe. For my sake.

He heard a voice say: "Very good. I'm printing this lot out. Your oncologist will be in a bit later. Relax."

I can do that, Mickey's Dad was thinking. I'm good at that. I can just lie back and let the world -

There was a crash.

Something had fallen on the floor. Mickey's Dad tried to prop himself up on his elbows, but he didn't have the strength. He could see a white coat out of the corner of his eye. Was it the first Doctor? The second? Or had he gone too?

The figure in the white coat spun around. He was holding something in his fist. He crashed it down on the stomach of the old man, the patient. Mickey's Dad doubled up, retching.

This is not like any treatment I'm used to, he was thinking.

Had the world gone mad?

Luckily, Mickey's Dad didn't need to wait for an explanation. He didn't have to know whether this was the other guy, Martin Something, or if he had been replaced. Or if someone else had come in, disguised in a white coat.

65

All he needed to know was that he was under attack.

He reacted, like the trained fighter he was.

He raised one arm and when the fist started down again, towards him, he blocked the blow, ran a hand along the arm and chopped at the man's elbow. The man screamed. He tried to pull back, but Mickey's Dad had his arm. Mickey's Dad levered himself with his legs over the edge of the bed. Now all he needed was his own weight and gravity.

He fell heavily on the floor and that took the wind out of him, but he still had an arm, and that was being bent backwards, not in the usual direction. Mickey's Dad was counting on the manoeuvre being excruciatingly painful.

The attacker screamed like he had been stabbed. He fell on the floor and Mickey's Dad rolled on top of him. Whatever weapon he had been able to use for the first swing was now gone. He was confronted with an experienced and ruthless opponent, someone with years of experience of being unforgiving and dirty in the clinch.

The man in the white coat grappled his way to his feet. Mickey's Dad let him go, knowing that the man would then have options. He could stay for Round Two or he could admit defeat and retreat. No problem. Dad would let him go.

There was scuffling and the white coat vanished. Seconds later, the porter came back into view. Horrified by what he saw, he helped the old man first to get upright and then stumble back into bed.

"A bit careless," he was muttering. "You could have hurt yourself."

He hadn't seen the attack, then. Mickey's Dad was philosophical. He had spent most of his life defending himself. It seemed that the whole world wanted a piece of him. Well, not today. He had scared the guy off.

When the oncologist came - later - he was alarmed to see that Mickey's Dad had a massive bruise, right in the middle of his stomach, just about on top of the site of the cancer. He tutted to himself, disapprovingly.

"You're not making my job any easier," he said, almost to himself.

Mickey's Dad, still woozy and a little out of it, let him mutter. He had far more important things to think about.

Later, when he was getting dressed, he looked at the scrap of material in his hand.

While the two men had been rolling around on the floor, Mickey's Dad had managed to clasp his hand on the attacker's clothing and he had pulled a piece off. He looked at it now, turning it over in his fingers.

It was a logo.

Well, Mickey's Dad was thinking with satisfaction, looks like I've got myself a clue.

* * * * *

Meanwhile, across town, Gibson's son was doing his own bit of sewing.

It wasn't much of a job. He was just working on something useful. A rucksack.

He wasn't proud of himself. I've just got to do it, he thought to himself. It's not for me, it's for my daughter. Surely no one could blame me for that. She's all I've got in the world. I have to do everything I can to save her life.

David, Gibson's son, wasn't very good at thinking. It wasn't his speciality.

The first thought that occurred to him was that his daughter needed specialised treatment, and money could buy the best. The second was that he had no money. The third was that he could blackmail people who had.

He'd dismissed the other option. That was the generous offer from his 'father', to put money his way. Oh sure, like Old Man Gibson had been his strongest supporter over the last few years. No, not at all. He's said he was sorry, but that was just words. No, if David wanted to be sure of getting cash, then he figured he would have to look elsewhere.

The Mayor of Greater Manchester. That was who he was going to ask.

David had already launched Phase One. That was the bomb on the tram, the one that exploded, nearly taking out Caulfield. Of course, the young man hadn't intended that. He had made the rucksack so that it was open at the top, and people would be able to see the wires poking out. He knew the Bomb Squad would be called. It would be an easy task for them to dismantle it, he was thinking. Unfortunately, when that idiot Caulfield lifted the bag, he must have shaken the trigger loose, which meant that, yes, it did go bang. If he'd just left it -

Still, the escapade had made the News, and that was all that really mattered.

Now, Phase Two was about to start. This one was going to be closer, and a whole lot more personal. It had to be. That was the only way, David concluded, that the politicians would think it was worthwhile handing over money.

He would have to make them scared, really scared. When they were quaking, they would pay.

David stood up and switched off the television on his way out.

Any observer, someone who could watch the young man day by day, would have seen that he spent far too long in front of the TV. Either that, or videos on his computer. One way or the other, he passed most of his waking hours absorbed in dramas that included murder, mayhem, blackmail and forensics. Crime and Thrillers were his staple diet, more regular an intake than food. It meant he had a terribly distorted view of Law and Order.

He was completely unrealistic. He lived in a fantasy world.

In that world, blackmail plans usually worked out - at least at first. Sure, the perpetrators were always caught in the end - every single time - but David thought he was too smart for that. I can make the threat, get the money and get away, he was thinking. They won't know what hit them. I'll have cash in my hands and my daughter will be saved.

God, I love a happy ending!

Less than an hour later he was walking down Oxford Street in the middle of Manchester. It was a cold but sunny day, and there was no sign of rain. Perfect for travelling, as well as planting bombs, he concluded. I can't lose.

His destination was a big old office building on one side of the road. He approached confidently, walked in through the revolving door and scanned the board on one side that listed tenants and the floor they were on.

Sure enough, it was all about Greater Manchester, the county he lived in.

The Waste Disposal Authority had two floors, apparently. The Transport Directorate had one. The Pension Fund was there, as well as the County Environmental Planning Department. There was more, something about travel.

The Mayor had an office near the top. Not quite the penthouse, David concluded, but close enough.

"Can I help you?" a voice said behind him.

David turned. A Commissionaire in smart uniform was hovering, checking this new arrival out.

"I've got an appointment," David declared and made his way towards the lifts.

But he didn't take the lift. For one thing, he hated confined spaces. Secondly, he had an awful vision pop into his head, and it involved the lift coming to an abrupt stop, too quickly, and setting off the sensitive mechanism he was carrying.

I'll take the stairs, he decided. That many floors? I need the exercise, he grinned to himself.

He did. He was out of condition. A life in front of telly, punctuated by the intake of various drugs, had destroyed whatever musculature he had gained growing up. By the time he reached the correct level, he was gasping for breath.

David paused, one hand on the rail by the stairs. He took great gulps of air. He was nearly shaking.

At last, partially recovered, he went through the door.

There was a clear sign, saying 'Mayor' and an arrow. Going in that direction, he was pleased to see a door marked 'Toilets'. That's for me, he decided, and went in.

It was Unisex. That was baffling. He had anticipated one marked 'Ladies' and one marked 'Gents', but No, it was first come, first served. He went in an unoccupied booth and closed the door behind him.

He'd seen this in the movies. Climb up on the toilet seat and raise the air duct over your head. Push your bag in to the tunnel, and lower the grille back into place. He did it. He did all that, pleased with himself.

I have achieved my aim, he was thinking to himself, as he washed his hands in the shared sinks.

Then new people came in.

It was a mother and daughter, young daughter. The kid was less than school age, and was chatting furiously, excited to be out and about in the big city and visiting the building where the Metro Mayor 'lived'. She was gabbling, practising her language. She liked the toilets too, the chrome and shiny sinks. She said so. Her mother indulged her.

David looked distraught.

He hadn't thought of this, hadn't realised that if his device actually went off then it might seriously injure people like they were - mother and child. A pretty woman, the same age as his deceased partner, the drug addict.

And a young girl, maybe the same age as his own.

It might be that he would destroy a young life, someone else's - in order to save the one he cared about most.

He hadn't thought it through.

*   *   *   *   *

Meanwhile, at the same time, up the same road, Melia was in The Trade Hotel for a second time.

She was visiting Gorange, again.

This time she had made it into his room, which was actually a different room to the one he had before. In fact, he moved rooms every day, sometimes twice a day. Careful, or paranoid? Maybe, Melia was thinking, it was the same thing.

But the visit wasn't going well.

The arch villain was looking a little off. His face, what there was left of it, was looking paler than usual, and he seemed to have trouble standing up straight. Was he ill? Did he have an infection? He seemed reluctant to answer direct questions, but half way through a mocking tirade, he excused himself and dashed to the toilet.

Not too impressive for a 'soldier of fortune', Melia was thinking.

The room was bigger than the last one, practically a suite. There were two easy chairs over by the window, but Melia couldn't sit still. She stood up and prowled the area, maybe looking for clues. What was Gorange up to?

On the table top, in front of a large mirror, there was a paper bag. She looked closer. In the bag was a cardboard box, about the size of - About the size of a hand gun, if she was being honest.

He had an extra weapon.

"Leave that alone!" he snarled wearily.

Melia turned. Gorange had a hand to his mouth, as if wiping away spit. He looked green, as if he had been sick.

"You look like death," she told him, without thinking.

"I will do, soon enough," he said.

They faced each other. Suddenly, there was a silence between them. What was he saying – and not saying? What was he hiding?

Gorange had always been a vain man, she knew. A proud man. He was struggling to stand straight, haughty, as ever, but it wasn't working for him. He seemed to have less muscle tone than before. He seemed to be stooped.

"I've told you I have cancer," he reminded her.

Melia nodded. His voice was now so rough, so low and rasping. It was like the words were being dragged out of him. But, hearing that, it just meant he sounded more authentic than usual. For once, he didn't seem to be lying.

"Don't worry," he said. "You know me. I'm not one for dragging out the drama. If the Docs can't cure me, I'll be only to eager to end it for myself. I don't plan on having a long goodbye."

Melia sighed. Yes, that was the explanation for all their interactions. The reality saddened her.

No, he hadn't come running because he was only too delighted to see her. No. He simply wanted to say Farewell.

She found herself staggering back. She came up against the bed, and sat down on it abruptly.

Well, there was one thing, she realised immediately. He hadn't said he loved her so that they would find some joy together. It was just something he wanted to get off his chest while he was able to.

She was just a loose end he was tying up before his own end.

"I'm sorry," she whispered, and knew that it was true. She really felt sorry for him.

He nodded, grateful for that, maybe, but not really keen to have her pity.

After a long pause, something occurred to Melia. That parcel.

"The box," she said. "A gun? You've got a pistol to use on yourself."

He frowned, turned, saw what she was looking at, and shook his head. He seemed to chuckle, just a little.

"No , not at all," he said, smiling at her naievity. "It's actually a healing device. I bought it from a man I met. He's famous in these parts, apparently. He runs clinics in local churches. One of my regular contacts tipped me off."

Melia had no idea what he was saying.

She jumped up, walked over and stood over him while he pulled off the paper bag and opened the box. There was a glistening, shiny object inside, with wires, like a charger, and some oil in a bottle.

"That's a 'healing device'?" she asked, baffled. She had never seen anything like it.

That would 'cure' him?

He sighed. "Yes, it is ridiculous," he agreed. "I have no idea whether it would do any good. I just don't know."

"You must use it!" she said, the words spilling out of her mouth. Her own vehemence surprised her.

"No, you must," she went on. "If there is the slightest chance it could do you some good, then you should!"

He looked at her, concerned. It was like something had risen to the surface.

So far, in their interactions, Melia had been distant, as if hiding behind a barrier, distancing herself from him. But now, something had been triggered. The sight of the machine had brought home to her everything he was saying. His life would end, he had said, as if putting the idea forward, and now she was actually convinced.

She couldn't stand the idea that he would be leaving her life.

"Take it out!" she said, and started helping. "Plug it in," she said. "Let's see how it works. Now, show me."

They read the instructions together, and he plugged it in, as she urged. Under such pressure, he did exactly what he was asked and pressed the 'Start' button. It hummed and he ran it over his chest.

"It says you have to do it every day," she said, the leaflet in her hand.

He had the device in one hand. The other he used to reach out and take hers. There were tears in his eyes.

"I didn't know you cared," he said softly, a little sarcastically but with all the gratitude he could find.

She took a breath. No, she didn't realise either.

Melia didn't know the contents of her own heart. She had been hiding her true feelings for so many years.

It was all new, an amazing surprise for the girl they called 'Heartless'.

7. CHAPTER SIX: Mistaken Identity

A couple of days later, Mickey's Dad was at Regional Office, in Terry's work room.

This time, the older man actually knew who the kid with the red hair actually was.

It was inevitable. When Mickey's Dad had been attacked in hospital, the police were called and the fact that the assault might involve somebody dressed as a Doctor and pretending to be one of the staff, alerted them to the possibility it could be a Security issue. The report had been copied to TEEF as a matter of routine. Terry picked it up, saw the familiar grizzled face of a parent he knew, and dialled up the CCTV. It was shocking.

I'll have to discuss it with the big guy, he decided.

It meant tracking down Mickey's Dad, again - he was in a different hotel by this time - then going and knocking on his door. Terry introduced himself, explained his previous interaction when playing the part of 'Salesman'. That was all a bit muddling, but as soon as he said he was a colleague of Mickey's, the Dad invited him in. Of course.

He wanted to hear all and any news about his son. They went to the hotel bar and had a session.

The next day Terry was nursing a hangover, but Mickey's Dad was made of sterner stuff.

"Let's get on with it," he urged.

They were sitting in a darkened room in front of a bank of computer monitors. Terry had managed to obtain copies from all the relevant cameras. He was able to show the old man arriving, then being issued with his hospital gown.

"Not my best side," Mickey's Dad commented, when they saw him sitting on the trolley.

Mickey's Dad was wheeled into the curtained-off cubicle and a doctor arrived and gave him an injection.

Winding on, the anaesthetist left and a second person in white coat came in to administer treatment.

"I didn't realise all this stuff was recorded," Dad said, surprise in his voice.

Terry grimaced. Yes, well, mainly it was because of the growing number of Malpractice lawsuits. The hospitals needed evidence they could show in court to prove that their staff had acted responsibly.

Sure, it was a shocking intrusion into somebody's personal business and would have been - if made public - embarrassing. But yes, it did save confusion and did help prevent those 'He says, you say' arguments.

There was a knock on the door.

Terry turned, puzzled. He wasn't expecting any visitors. He was about to stand, open it, when it burst open.

End of confusion. It was Jeremy Ceremony.

Terry and Mickey's Dad both froze. They had the advantage of the new arrival: they knew who he was.

He didn't know either of them from Adam, (even though he had 'treated' the old man, once, in the Big Top).

"I hear you're looking into Martin Muffin," Jermy said. "I have a complaint about him."

Terry was standing stock still. He had never been near the healer, so wasn't expecting his lopsided face. The accident, he was thinking. I read about his car crash, when I was doing the research. It looks pretty bad, close up.

Mickey's Dad was made of sterner stuff. He'd seen worse injuries, some when they were new. Still, in the brief moments he had been sitting in the chair on the night of the Big Healing, he hadn't got a close look at his helper. Plus, there were spotlights coming from every angle, dimming the vision, maybe it difficult to see anything.

Terry recovered.

"Whoa, Whoa, Whoa," he said, coming to his senses. "How the hell did you get in here?"

He was referring to Regional Office. God dammit, it was meant to be secret! Was it actually 'Open House' to any old fraudster? Wouldn't they stop him at the Front Desk? Mr Cermoney had no clearance, no valid documentation.

"I know Melia," the man said calmly.

Mickey's Dad guffawed, a hoarse laugh that indicated total disbelief. Terry just seemed puzzled again.

"She bought an ultrasound device from me," the two men were told. "She said she needed it for 'a friend'. Yeah?"

Terry had no idea whether it was true, or yet another fantasy from this prolific talker. He shrugged, then pulled out a chair. Whatever the facts, he would have to take up the issues later. Right now, they had a task to fulfil.

"We're looking at Martin Muffin in action," he said.

Jermy sat down between the two men and tried to focus on the screen.

Actually, the action had wound on while they were going through the introductions. The bits that covered Mickey's Dad having ultrasound treatment had passed and that visitor had moved out of the area.

Terry hit the 'fast forward' button, and then the next man came into the room, dressed in a white coat.

"That's Martin Muffin," Jermy said, delighted.

"No, that's my attacker," Mickey's Dad said, correcting him.

"Yes, he attacked me," Jermy agreed. "Well, verbally, but the situation was ugly. It happened outside St Cyprian's church in Salford. I go there and administer treatments. Mr Muffin seems to resent that and wants me to stop."

"He tried to stop me," Mickey's Dad agreed.

The looked at the screen. It reached the point where Dad and the intruder were rolling around on the floor. Then the attacker scrambled to his feet, fighting off hands that grabbed for him. He vanished out of the cubicle.

"You let him go!" Jermy said, accusingly. "He's a dangerous man. You know that. Well, I felt it too. That's why I'm here. You need to get this man off the street. He could really do some damage. I don't know what I've done to upset him."

"Wait a minute, wait a minute," Terry said. "There's something not right here." He started to rewind the recording.

"I'm not like you," Jermy said to the old man. "I wouldn't be able to fight him off like you did. If he got physical with me, that would be the end. I mean, I gave him the option. I told him I would accept money. He's made no offer, yet."

Terry tapped some buttons. He was getting irritated with Jermy. Everything the fellah said made no sense.

"Right," he said, selecting a part of the video. "Now, you look at this," he said to him.

Jermy looked, but didn't seem interested. Terry and Mickey's Dad were nodding. They'd seen it before. It was the early part when the man who called himself Martin Muffin came in and started treating Dad with an ultrasound device.

"Look closely," Terry said to Mr Cermoney. "Now you tell me who that is."

"I can't. I've never seen him before in my life."

Terry tutted in frustration. He opened a drawer and pulled out a print-out of an article from a scholarly journal. There was a photo of the author at the top left of the page. His name was beside it. The implication was clear.

"THAT is Dr Muffin," Terry said. "From the Institute." It was the same man currently on the video.

"I don't know him," Jermy repeated. "He's not the man I met, the one who attacked me."

"He's not the one who attacked me," Mickey's Dad said, as if clarifying the problem in his own mind. "But it looks like the man who DID attack me is the same one who attacked you, Mr Cermoney. That's right, isn't it?"

Terry slapped the paper on his desk, and looked at what was in front of him.

He had two people, each feeling threatened. The video from the hospital showed an actual fight, and Mr Cermoney was here to complain about a possible fight looming. Terry had to make sense of that.

Meanwhile, yes, there was a real Dr Muffin, the man DID exist, and was active at Salford Hospital. In fact, he had administered treatment to Mickey's Dad. Should Terry be asking if that was successful?

Hopefully, it would be, because Mickey's Dad had only one other hope for a long life, and that was if the only other person they both knew who worked with ultrasound would be able to help him fight his life-threatening disease.

And that was the only other guy here, a certain Jeremy Something - a self-declared, healing 'genius'.

* * * * *

At about the same time, Melia was back at St Cyprian's church. Again.

She was standing outside, hesitating to go in.

This is ridiculous, she was thinking. She couldn't understand her mixed feelings.

Why? The last time she had been there it was precisely to find a certain 'asylum seeker' and recent returnee to this country. She had an old photo of him, and left a copy with the Vicar. So, when she got the phone call -

Melia couldn't understand it. She wanted the woman to call, didn't she? It was just what she was waiting for. The message was that the man had returned, and been seen in the area. The Minister wanted Melia to come down and talk about it. Maybe the Reverend Karney would know who had spotted the man. Maybe she would let Melia talk to them.

What was the problem?

Well, firstly, it was the way that the previous visit had ended. It had been blown apart by a telephone call arriving out of the blue asking for Jeremy Somebody. It had completely derailed Melia, thrown her off her focus. Something about it -

Of course, looking from the outside, an observer might note that the episode was the last time Melia had heard of the man, or had any info from people dealing with him. The fact was she didn't know that Terry the technician, or Captain Gibson, her boss, had occasion to see and interact with him. She didn't know either of them had any reason to, since the Director hadn't seen fit to share his state of health with any of his employees thus far.

More pertinent, Melia hadn't, at this stage, met with or had any conversation with the other person Terry was dealing with, that is, Mickey's Dad. In point of fact, if anyone had asked Melia if Mickey had a Dad -

Well, there was a lot she didn't know.

Actually, the only thing she did know, at that point, was that Gorange, her old adversary, was saying to her that he had cancer. He was the only person that had said it to her, and he was the only one who told her that he had purchased a 'healing device'. She didn't know anyone else who had one and had never seen one in action anywhere else.

No, that wasn't it.

It wasn't the way the interview had ended, she realised. It was the way it was going when it stopped.

The fact was, Melia concluded, that she hadn't actually taken a liking to the woman Priest. For some reason, and in ways that she couldn't explain, the lady had rubbed her up the wrong way. They just didn't get along.

That much would have been obvious too - to the same outside observer - because for the rest of the time that Melia was on the premises that day - and that night - Melia had been happy to help - make beds, ladle out soup, make tea and burn toast - but had studiously avoided doing any of it with the Vicar. She had not gone near the woman, at all.

Finally, last piece of evidence, although Melia had promised the Priest that she would help out in future with the homeless people, and would be a regular volunteer, she had managed to find a whole series of reasons why she was far 'too busy' to go back for a return session. She felt guilty about that, realising that those poor unfortunates needed all the help they could get - even if it was from a less than caring spy - but she hadn't kept in touch.

The phone call, therefore, was a complete surprise.

Melia took a deep breath. I've got a job to do, she decided. I'm a professional. I've got a man to catch.

"She's not here," the verger said.

Melia was overwhelmed by the biggest feeling of relief she had felt in weeks. She was actually pleased when the church official told her that the Vicar was out 'visiting the sick'.

He wanted to be helpful, this man, and when Melia explained that she needed to 'have a look around', he simply waved a hand, and welcomed her in.

"You're some kind of police person," he whispered conspiratorially, sizing her up.

"Some kind," she agreed.

Let him think what he liked, she thought, nodding. He was a middle-aged, jovial man, good with people and pleased to be doing good. He said he had 'enough to do' in the kitchen, getting ready for the evening influx. Melia could prowl around as much as she wanted. Melia thanked him and agreed to join him for a cup of tea, later.

In truth, she had little idea what she should do.

The lady Priest had told her that the man, the one she was looking for, had 'been seen'. Did that mean he was nearby now? Did it mean he would be back that night? The homeless people weren't allowed to store any of their possessions on the premises. There would be no lockers to search, no cupboards to go through. In fact, nobody to talk to.

Melia went past the door to the kitchen, past the double doors that opened out into the body of the church, and approached the doors that led off to the Day Room, where overnight visitors were fed, and various activities took place during the day, such as the Sewing Group, and the Women's Institute.

She heard voices from inside. Well, just call in and say Hello, she was thinking.

She opened the door.

Melia wasn't sure what she was looking at. There were a dozen people standing either side of a long table, and there were clothes, bags and shoes spread out all along it. There was an animated discussion going on, but it stopped.

A lady looked up and smiled. Melia recognised her as one of the volunteers who worked with the homeless.

"Just sorting the Jumble," she said brightly. The homeless people needed a change of clothes, sometimes. People donated stuff to the church and the volunteers put it into categories for them to choose. Different sizes, indoor and outdoor clothes, shoes and socks. There were all kinds of things that homeless people needed.

Melia nodded, but said she 'was busy'. She walked through the room and out the far door, into the Store Room.

This was where the beds were kept, when they weren't being used. Also, blankets, pillows and the rest.

Melia closed the door behind her. She didn't need to be there, but she wanted a chance to think.

Something was off.

Slowly, it dawned on her. The volunteers - Yes, some of them were the church 'regulars' she had met, when she did her stint. But also, well, she had met some of the others too. She recognised the faces.

They were some of the clients. The homeless people.

But they weren't allowed in the church during the day! It was a strict policy. What on earth were they doing there?

Melia looked around. Cupboards. Drawers. Closets. Wardrobes.

Suddenly, she felt very suspicious.

She pulled open cupboard doors. She saw pillows and bedding. Then she saw coats and woolly jumpers, neatly folded and stacked. Then trousers and socks. All for the clients, yes, that was right. Second-hand clothes.

Then the next cupboard. Clothes, yes, but new. New? Some still in wrappers, unopened. Some with logos.

Then the next door, a small one, near the floor.

Melia staggered back, completely flummoxed by what she found. It can't be! What did it mean? Rows of shelves, and all full of the same thing, over and over, different colours but stacked neatly and folded. Waiting.

Rucksacks.

* * * * *

Later that same day, in the evening, Captain Gibson went looking for his son, at the scabby flat where he chose to live.

Mr Gibson toiled up the stairs. Why do lifts never work in these old blocks? he wondered. He was breathing heavily when he reached the right floor. It made him sad. Years ago - until quite recently - he could have bounded up the staircases. Something had happened to his health. He seemed to have lost the edge.

He counted off the doors until he came to the one he had visited before, where he had found his estranged 'son'.

The door was slightly open.

Not wanting to be rude, he plonked the knocker several times. Then leaned into the gap and called out, 'David'.

No reply.

He pushed the door. It creaked back noisily on rusted hinges, and hung open mournfully. A stench wafted out.

Gibson called out, again, then again. When there was no sound, no reply, no challenge, he walked in.

It was desperately sad. The places was so badly maintained, dirty and overrun with rubbish. How could any sane human live in a dump like this? he wondered. What did I do to make the kid so mean? Gibson regretted every lost year.

"Hey, moke!" a voice called out, behind him.

There were three of them. They wore so much jewellery, gold chains and exposed bare arms, they might as well have had the words 'Drug Dealer' tattooed across their foreheads. They were all young, all male, all ugly.

"Grandpa," the middle one said, "Where's David?"

"You family?" the second one said, not giving time for a reply to the first question.

Gibson considered. "You want me to answer the first question first, or maybe - "

"If you don't belong here," the third one said, "you'd better move on."

Gibson nodded. He had no reason to engage the youngsters in conversation. If they wanted David, it wasn't his concern. He would move right along, as suggested. He could always call back another day.

"If you've got business here," the second one went on, "then you must be family."

That didn't make sense, either, Gibson was thinking. Still, he wasn't responsible for education in the country.

"I didn't get an answer," the first one said, which was true. He had a knife in his hand. He moved closer.

The knife clattered to the floor.

The young man looked at it, then looked at his wrist, which was now growing an ugly red bruise.

He looked baffled. Something had happened, he reasoned, but he hadn't seen a thing.

Gibson was breathing steadily, not bothered. If they want to try it on, he was thinking, I will defend myself.

The kid, grumbling, reached down to retrieve his weapon. He flew backwards across the room.

The second had to jump sideways to avoid getting flattened. It didn't please him.

"Now, look," he said threateningly, "if you're going to get tasty - "

Gibson said: "I think you'll find that he attacked me first."

The kid had run out of conversation. Without another word, he launched himself across the room, screaming.

Gibson waited, then stepped to one side. The attacker flew into the space he had just vacated, found no resistance, and continued on his path, until he flattened himself against the far wall. He slid down it, with a sigh.

The third dealer had a more workmanlike approach. He advanced on Gibson slowly, determinedly. He raised a fist, drew it back, then flung it forward with all his might. It stopped in mid-air, when it came up against Gibson's palm.

The Captain stood waiting. When the kid didn't respond, he simply turned his wrist on its axis.

The youngster squealed with pain, and would have continued, but there was a crack. It silenced him.

"This has gone on long enough," the first one said coldly, from his place over by the door.

He was standing still and his right arm was extended. There was a gun in that hand.

Gibson took a breath. The fight might have ended there, then, and he would have come off worst.

But a strange thing happened. A hand appeared over the gang leader's shoulder. It clamped down on the gun and pushed it in an arc, right into the gunman's body. There was the muffled sound of a shot, and the young man collapsed.

Gibson stared at the newcomer. He was as ancient as himself and had salt and pepper hair.

"I'm obliged," he said politely.

"I'm Mickey's Dad," the well-built newcomer told him.

Gibson grinned. He actually smiled, which was unusual for him.

"Then we have one thing in common," he admitted.

"We need to talk," the other said, moving forward.

As there was an ex-gunfighter laid flat out on the floor, nursing his stomach, Mickey's Dad was forced to walk right over him. Right over, from toes to head. The young man, already suffering broken fingers and a gunshot wound, found out what it was like to have one hundred and seventy pounds of muscle grind down on his groin and chest. Several ribs seemed to give way.

"How did you find me?" Gibson asked jovially.

"I've been spending time with your man Terry," the new arrival told him. "He said he always knows where to find you."

"Ah, I'll have to work on that," the Captain admitted. "The magic of mobile phones. They follow you everywhere."

"Modern technology," Mickey's Dad agreed. "That's about where my interest lies."

"You looking to solve a problem?"

"I'm looking for a cure," the old man confessed.

8. CHAPTER   SEVEN:
Misunderstandings

The next day, Jeremy arrived back at his regular church, anxious to heal the sick.

Unfortunately, his definition of 'sick' encompassed just about every strata and cranny of society. It went way beyond the simple illnesses such as cancer and diabetes. No, Jermy was convinced that his method could cure anything.

Even homelessness.

It was early afternoon. There was sun in the sky, but it was still early in the year and Spring hadn't arrived properly yet. Jermy was wearing a padded jacket, done up tight, and a woollen scarf. He was carrying a plastic shopping bag, which contained one of his ultrasound devices, as well as the attachments and oils. (He hadn't seen the kit that Terry had constructed, with its neat arrangement and hard covered case, so didn't know that his system could be improved with better packaging. But even if he had known, he probably would have disapproved. He wanted 'accessibility', he often said.)

The gates to the churchyard were open and the outer doors of the church were unlocked. The place was open. That particular afternoon there was nothing special going on - such as the Karate Club or the Slimming Group - but when the place was open, people often popped in, looking for a cup of something and some convivial chat.

Jermy pushed through the doors and was surprised to see the Sewing Group were there.

He knew the people, mostly women. Many of them also came along to the Monday group, the gathering at the start of the week, launching people into the workaday world after a lazy weekend. That was the meeting that Jermy valued the most. People had always been welcoming to him there. He found them open, and happy to talk about illness and disease.

The Sewing Group was far more intense. They always seemed as if they were on a mission. They usually had their table full of oddments and scraps, and were forever piecing together new dresses and skirts. It wasn't an interest of his. He preferred his clothes ready-made, and couldn't see the point of what they were doing. Still, they also made scarves, and it was cold -

"You looking for Rev?" one of the younger women said, seeing Jermy enter. "She's out."

"No, no," he told her. "I'm happy to see you. All of you. I've just come in for a chat? How's the back, Pat?"

The woman called Pat looked uncomfortable to be asked. But, thinking about it, she appreciated that the treatment Jermy had given her several weeks before may actually have worked. A little. She did feel better. A bit.

"Don't worry about me," she snapped, a little irritated at being singled out. "This is the man you need to help."

Jermy turned. Yes, a man, sitting on the end of the table. He had needle and thread in his hands, but it wasn't obvious what he was working on. Some kind of bag? Jermy smiled, since he always tried to be upbeat.

"You have a problem?" he asked brightly. "Something I can help you with?"

"I have no home," the young man told him. "But I also have the pain in shoulder."

He had a thick accent and a strange way with words. Jermy wasn't bothered about that. He would help anybody.

He plugged the device into the nearest power socket and told the man to pull his chair closer, so that he would be in reach. The man put down his sewing. He was looking questioningly at the women, but they all waved him on.

"It might help," Pat said. "Give it a try, son. He can't kill you."

"He might wanna try!" another woman said, laughing.

They all seemed to find that terribly funny. Jermy wasn't laughing. He just wanted to help people.

He had the man sitting on the chair now, near the wall so that the electrical cord would stretch. He told him to take his jacket off, then ran the device along his collar bone and around his shoulder blades. The man grunted.

Jermy said: "Our external circumstances are a reflection of our inner world."

The man looked doubtful, but Jermy was being serious. He truly believed that if he treated this fellow properly, with the full treatment, then his condition of homelessness would resolve, as easily as his shoulder pain.

"What in God's name is going on here?" a loud, intrusive voice bellowed from the door.

It was the Vicar. She had arrived. She was less than pleased at what she was seeing.

"I've told you before - " she stormed. "Get out! Get out!"

"I'm trying to assist - " Jermy began, determined to continue.

The woman priest strode over and switched the power off at the socket. She pulled out the plug and flung it at Jermy in disgust. She was fuming. All the women could see she meant business. They weren't laughing now.

"My church," the Vicar said. "My rules!"

Jermy tried to make a dignified exit, but the priest stood over him while he packed his bag, then hustled him out the door and into the yard. She stood with folded arms, daring him to argue. He was defeated.

"You'll never admit what I can do," Jermy said plaintively.

He was upset. This place had once been a haven for him. People had welcomed him in. He felt protected.

"You think you can heal the sick - " she began.

"Better than your version!"

The Vicar looked at him, lost for words. Was he referring to Bible stories? Her Lord cured the sick while he was on Earth. It was even said he raised the dead. Was Jermy daring to put himself even slightly into the same category?

Jermy said: "You should see my leaflets. It says, 'JC's Cure for Cancer'. That's me. I'm JC, and I've got a system that works. Not like your JC. With you, it's all fantasy and fairy stories, passed down through many generations."

"My 'JC'?" she gasped. "Who?"

"Jesus Christ."

The Vicar screamed.

The cry was sucked out of her. She had never heard such blasphemy! In former years, such outright heresy and disrespect might have earned him a place at a burning stake. She couldn't believe her ears.

"You are daring to compare yourself - " she yelled.

Jermy turned, as if thinking about going.

It was beginning to dawn on him that he might have gone too far, but somehow he couldn't stop himself.

"We know," he said abruptly, "what YOUR JC's 'Cure for Cancer' is. It's death. That's all you can offer, isn't it? Believe in religion, and it will kill you. Still, why worry? You will go to a 'better place', won't you? That's what you believe."

"Get out!" the priest shouted, as loud as her lungs could manage. "Get off this property and never desecrate it again!"

"I'm going," Jermy mumbled. "You people, you can't handle the truth."

"Your truth is not my truth," she told him, yelling it at his retreating back.

Jermy walked up the road, feeling sad. I wanted to say it, he was thinking. I've wanted to say it, for a long time.

Still, he was sorry. He was thinking, it looks like I've burned my bridges there.

*   *   *   *   *

At about the same time, Terry was in his room at Regional Office, trying to contact Mickey.

It should have been simple. Mickey was on assignment, on a mission, directed by the Department. He had been deputed from the Unit, and taken passage out through London, but it should have meant that he was at least contactable, no matter where in the world he was now. He had to keep in touch, didn't he? Whether in the jungle, desert or ocean.

Mickey didn't reply. Well, he didn't 'pick up'. Maybe he was sleeping, Terry thought, and left a message. He was quite clear. He said that Mickey's Dad was 'in Manchester' and was wanting to meet him. Those were the words.

While he was waiting for Mickey to get back to him, Terry idled his time away by looking up Mickey's Dad's Service record. That was easy enough, anyway. The computer clicked, beeped a bit and there it was.

My, a real hero!

Yes, Mickey's Dad had an impressive career. He had served in many theatres, earned a few mentions and been nominated for medals. Most of what he did was far too discreet to allow such public commendations, but his superior officers had filed reports, confidentially, and they were glowing in their praise. He was a fine soldier, no doubt about it.

But that had abruptly stopped. All that, the fine words, was before the Dad went for a routine medical and found he had cancer. After it, all hell broke loose.

First, the old man quit. No waiting around for retirement, he just walked out.

Then, to make matters worse, he started taking on 'outside' work, freelance jobs. They were often the most risky and unpopular missions. Most of them would be classed as 'suicidal'. Mickey's Dad took them all on.

He doesn't care, Terry was thinking. He knows he's going to die and it makes him fearless.

Terry admired that, even if the recklessness and lack of discipline was something he would normally disapprove of.

But Terry was smarting. He'd had a recent run-in -

Terry squirmed to even think about it. It was all so stupid!

It started with a car drive. Terry didn't own a car, but he could drive and he sometimes took out one of the Unit's cars. Most of those were big and muscular, and not really his style. Terry was more in love with something more modern, more futuristic. The electric car. Accordingly, he joined the 'Green Getters Car Club' in Bury. It was a short ride on the tram, up to the town north of Manchester, and a short walk out of the tram station to the depot. He'd booked a car for the afternoon recently. He was thinking of going to Blackburn. It was a short trip up the M66 motorway, and would allow him time to go back and forth on the M65, a notably scenic rural route. He wanted to really show up the car's paces.

He got the car, drove north up the M66, then off onto the dual carriageway, the A56, and on to the M65. It was a nice day, there was sun and blue sky, and the car just bowled along, with very little sound from its electric motor.

Terry was having fun. He went west on the M65, up to the M61 roundabout. He went right round the junction, and came back, heading east. Then, seeing Junction 5, he thought of the country road down through Haslingden, an alternative way of getting back to the M66. It was a nice road, very countryfied, with reservoirs on one side and wind turbines along the tops of the hills. It was pleasant to drive, and he steered that way.

The problem, as he quickly came to see, was that the narrow road twisted and turned and went through a succession of villages. The speed limit kept changing. First it was 50 miles per hour, then down to 40, and maybe even 30 in the built-up areas. He was having to check the signs every hundred yards. It was fast, slow, fast, slow. Very frustrating.

Coming down the hill, he came round a bend and saw the sign for 30. He applied the brakes.

There was a blast of horn behind him.

Looking in his rear-view mirror, Terry saw a red van behind him. Very close behind him. The driver was shaking a fist at him, as if very annoyed. Terry looked up. No, there was definitely a speed limit. Didn't the man see that? Did the man want him to cheat?

Terry drove responsibly, keeping to the speed allowed.

When he came out of that village, the sign said 50, so he speeded up. The van was right behind him - only a few yards behind him - all the way. For the next few miles the van was poised behind him, as if anxious to overtake. But it couldn't overtake, the road was far too narrow and twisting. There were no straight places to pass.

Terry drove around the corner and down the hill, and came to the motorway junction. He turned right and headed up the ramp, back on to the M66. There were two lanes, but the van couldn't overtake. It was uphill and the red vehicle clearly didn't have the power. Terry drove steadily on, but when the motorway started downhill, he was alarmed to hear the whooshing of a vehicle close to him. It was the red van, rushing past. It vanished off down the slope.

Terry took a deep breath. He didn't know what to think.

Maybe the other driver thought he had some complaint. Terry's driving had caused him problems? Terry considered. He'd only followed the rules of the road. If he had gone any faster, it would have been illegal.

Still, the red van had gone. It was out of his life. He started driving down the M66 back towards Bury.

But that didn't work. That particular motorway is quite up and down. It goes through hills and valleys. Sure, the red van had roared off into the distance, and Terry could see it there, far off. But when the road started uphill, Terry was alarmed to see himself catching up. The van was slowing down? It was certainly having trouble with the hills.

Terry eased back on the throttle. He wanted to keep his distance. He didn't want to let that driver think he was following him. The man was a speed freak. Let him go ahead, Terry was thinking. I don't want a confrontation.

But he got it.

After a few miles, he came to the turn-off to Bury. This was his stop. He hit the off ramp and started down. The red van was nowhere in sight. It had gone off into the distance? He had lost it at last?

Terry approached the traffic lights at the bottom of the slope and stared in disbelief. The red van was there, waiting at the lights. The lights were on red. Terry would have to stop too. There was only one car between him and the van.

Terry slowed, suddenly feeling fearful. He tried to hang back. Then the lights turned to green and the red van pulled forward. Terry still went slow, knowing the junction, knowing that the lights were only the first set on the roundabout. There were more. Sure enough, they eased forward twenty yards and then had to stop again. More red lights.

The red van was in the middle lane. Terry was pulling up behind it, slowly, cautiously. The van abruptly pulled out left and got into the left-hand lane, right in front of the lights. Terry took a sigh of relief. He would need to stay in the middle lane to get round to Bury. Maybe the van was going somewhere else.

The van door opened.

Terry stared in disbelief. The driver was out in the road, and was waving his fist.

Did he want a fight?

What was he trying to say? What had Terry done? Why was he the bad guy?

Then the lights changed. The traffic started moving. The cars behind the red van started peeping their horns. The driver got back in his vehicle and roared off, sticking to the outside lane, which took him back onto the motorway again. Gone. He was out of Terry's life. Terry carried on around the roundabout, through another set of lights and towards Bury. He took the car back to the depot and caught the tram back towards Manchester, and Regional Office in Salford.

He couldn't get it out of his mind.

It wasn't as if he really thought he would be attacked by the van driver, but the confrontation had shaken him up, more than he wanted it to. The aggression had been so real, so palpable. He couldn't believe it had escalated so much, from such a simple thing. Was it 'road rage'? Is that what they called it?

Above all, could he have done anything different?

The workroom door opened.

Terry looked up from his screen, and was surprised - but not upset - to see Melia.

"A little bird tells me you're trying to contact Mickey," she said, plumping herself down in a chair.

She wasn't looking great. Not having Mickey around was always something to upset her.

"I'm trying to get a message to him," Terry admitted.

"Well, get MY message to him. Tell him I miss him, and I want to talk."

Terry obediently tapped out the words. Nothing happened. He wasn't expecting an immediate response.

Melia wanted to talk some more. She didn't feel she could share her turmoil over Gorange with anyone in the Unit, so she talked about St Cyprian's church, and the problems she was having finding a certain person who was going under the disguise of an 'asylum seeker' and was a possible trouble maker. Terry nodded, and sympathised.

His computer beeped.

"What does it say?" Melia demanded, and looked over his shoulder.

Terry stared, dumbfounded. He couldn't mean -

"It's not for you," he blathered to Melia.

It was a previous communication, he tried to say. Another person. He doesn't mean you. Honestly.

Melia was looking at the screen, and tears came to her eyes. She looked genuinely hurt to see the message.

It read: 'I don't care'.

* * * * *

Meanwhile, Deputy Director Caulfield was tackling another important mission, out in the field. Again.

He had been chosen - over all rivals - to be the one who would meet with the 'Blackmailing Bomber' and hand over the cash. All on behalf of the Metro Mayor, who had responded promptly. Unlike previous victims, he wasn't 'refusing to deal with' threats. On the contrary, he decided on an immediate response, and told his staff to fetch the money from the nearest bank.

"Only one thing," he told Captain Gibson. "You hand over the money, disarm the bomb, then capture the bomber."

That's three things, the Director was thinking uncharitably, but didn't say it.

Unfortunately, he didn't have enough staff available to mount a risk-free stakeout.

"You meet the person," he told Caulfield, "and trip your alarm. Don't worry, we'll come running."

Caulfield shook his head. That sounded a pretty half-hearted plan, he was thinking.

Little did he know - or anyone else - that the threat was coming from none other than Mr Gibson's son David.

Perhaps if he'd known that - Well, if Gibson had known that - there might have been more resources.

Unfortunately, the day of the handover was also a busy time for the elected County Mayor. It was the day of his 'Green Summit', a day he had been planning for months. He was going to use the occasion to announce all kinds of new initiatives - electric cars; Pure Air zones; bicycle lanes; local vegetable planting; phasing out plastics in canteens. It promised to be a great day, and was a magnet for the region's media.

Maybe that was why the bomber was happy to choose it. Perhaps he thought he would be lost in the crowd.

He was.

The Mayor's Office got the first phone call just before mid-day, to say that the handover would occur 'on the First Floor' of the Convention Centre in the middle of Manchester. Unfortunately, even as Caulfield got in place, the first session ended in the Main Hall and six hundred delegates came spilling out, looking for lunch.

Deputy Director Caulfield, wearing his usual smart suit, added to by the placement of a red rose in his lapel - at the bomber's request - was totally obscured by the milling throng. He tried to find a vantage point, then phoned in to say he was 'at the top of the stairwell', overlooking the foyer. He hadn't looked at the timetable for the day. He didn't know that once people had grabbed their plates of food, they would be heading upstairs to the Exhibition Rooms, where dozens of groups and organisations had set up tables, stalls and displays, advertising their services.

Caulfield was overwhelmed again.

The poor man found himself literally 'swimming against the tide', as he tried to get back downstairs.

By the time he found a quiet corner and phoned the Mayor's Office, he was shaking with anxiety and tension. The briefcase in his mitt, containing the thousands of pounds in small denomination notes, was weighing him down.

Terry answered his call. He was a familiar and reassuring voice.

"We've had an update from the bad guy," he told his boss. "He admits he couldn't find you at the Convention Centre, so he's come up with a new plan. He will meet you here, at the Mayor's office."

"That will be a lot safer," Caulfield agreed. "It's a cattle market here."

"Oh, yeah. 'Safe'. Yeah. The guy says that's where the bomb is, in this building."

Caulfield walked out of the Convention Centre and got back onto the street. He walked up towards the tramlines, then turned right and went down the road. It didn't take him more than ten minutes to get to the right place.

He walked in, saw the Mayor's Office listed on the notice board of tenants and noted the floor. He started up the staircase - he didn't want to get stuck in the lift, even if that was only a faint chance of something going wrong.

Caulfield turned up the last flight of stairs. The door banged open behind him and he felt a jab in the back.

"Don't turn around!" a voice demanded.

The Deputy Director stood stock still, waiting for further instructions.

I have been intercepted, he was thinking. I haven't even made it to the Office. They don't know I'm here.

"The money," the voice said. "Hand it over."

"I need to see the bomb first," Caulfield told him.

Caulfield was impressed with himself. He sounded quite confident, even though he had no idea what he was doing.

The bomber seemed to think about that, considering the implications. Then he said: "Next floor."

The Deputy Director carried on climbing. When he reached the next floor, he waited, and the harsh voice behind him told him to go through the door. They walked into a lobby, and the next instruction was to enter the toilet on the left.

Caulfield was breathing heavily, partly from the strain of climbing stairs, but also from the stress of dealing with a possible killer. He hadn't even seen the guy's face. He wouldn't be able to identify him then, if he was asked.

"The bomb is in the ceiling," Caulfield was told, but the man with the money was on a roll.

"Show me," he insisted.

The bomber came round the front. He was wearing a ski mask, so his face was totally obscured. He was wearing baggy clothes, jeans and a sweater, so it was impossible to gauge his build. He had no distinguishing features.

Caulfield had the satisfaction of seeing the young man climb on top of a toilet and push the ventilation panel to one side, so that he could see the bomb. Yes, it had wires. He had seen something like it before. On a tram.

The kid climbed down, leaving the thing showing.

"Now," he said. "The money."

The cash was in a briefcase and the case was handcuffed to the Deputy Director's wrist. He made a great show of unlocking it, then raised the case. I can't hand it over, he was thinking. I need to save it and arrest this guy.

The youth was too quick for him. Before Caulfield could say anything further, the case was seized from his hand and he was pushed off balance. The bomber scuttled out of the door, and it slammed behind him. By the time Mr Caulfield had got to his feet and got out of the toilet, the lobby was empty. Villain and money, all gone.

Caulfield's phone rang. It was Terry.

"I've got the Bomb Squad on the line," he told his boss. "They'll talk you through. You have to defuse the bomb."

Caulfield smiled. A dangerous job, he was thinking, but if I succeed, then maybe people will forget the fact I lost the money and the perpetrator. It's not all doom and gloom then. Not a total failure of a day.

With any luck, Caulfield was thinking, I could be a hero. Again.

9.   CHAPTER EIGHT: Ruthless

That night, somebody tried to kill Mickey's Dad.

He had taken precautions. He appeared to check in to The Trade Hotel for another night, but he did what he'd done before and went out of the back door and on up the road. He then checked in to another small hotel, around the back of The Bridgewater Hall, the concert venue. Then he walked out of that. An hour later, he was going in the back door of the Temple.

It was an old haunt.

Not everybody knew that The Sacred Society had bedrooms on the top floor of their premises. Most members only ever saw the ceremonial rooms on the ground floor, and the Bar of course, and sometimes the massive Dining Room. Yes, there was all that, and the small Museum on the second floor. But as well as that, senior members were allowed to stay overnight. There was plenty of space and nice, well-appointed, en-suite rooms, just for the chosen few.

Mickey's Dad was one of them. He didn't advertise the fact, and it had all happened by accident. But once, on an undercover mission, he was playing the part of man who joined the Society. When he came back to 'real life', he was surprised to find his membership was still acknowledged. Well, it was useful. He didn't hand in his card.

There was a scuffling sound at the door.

It wasn't much, but it was enough to wake Mickey's Dad, who spent most of his adult life on a hair trigger.

He stirred uneasily, listening. Whoever it was, they were fiddling with the lock, which meant they'd managed to get hold of a key from somewhere. Either through bribery or intimidation, they had managed to discover a way to gain entry without actually battering the door down and causing a fuss. Mickey's Dad smiled to himself.

Ah, professionals, he was thinking.

The fact was, at that particular moment, he wasn't really sure who was after him. It had been a number of organisations over the years, and a number of Security Services from a selection of different countries. Right now - Well, who wanted his hide? He'd lost count of those who had tried and failed. Who was still trying? That was the question.

The first man eased the door open.

The corridor was in darkness, mostly, but there was an Emergency bulb, down by the lift, so it was possible to see the man's shadow against the doorway. Similarly, it would have been possible to see the other outline, another man, standing behind the first. Mickey's Dad had deliberately left a chink of window curtain open, so that a small amount of light came in to the room from the street outside. That was a regular ploy; it meant that any 'visitor' would be facing a space brighter than the one they were moving out of, and it would place them at a disadvantage. Their eyes would have to adjust.

The first man had one hand outstretched and that hand had a gun in it. He took two steps forward and fired a shot.

It was impressive. The gun was silenced. That's never as easy as it looks in the movies - Mickey's Dad knew that - but these guys had taken the trouble to get the best equipment. It was cold, and efficient.

The body in the bed moved, and the gunman fired again. It had a similar effect.

Thinking his job was done, he advanced forward boldly.

He was surprised, therefore, when he cleared the bathroom door and the wardrobe and came into the main part of the room, that a figure came out of the shadows on his left and seized his arm. He wasn't expecting that.

He assumed the mass under the bedclothes was Mickey's Dad, the intended target. He hadn't guessed that it would be a bolster of pillows and spare blankets, stuffed into shape. He didn't think that Mickey's Dad would be in a chair beside the wall, dozing, and would then - having waited for his entrance - explode at him with such force.

The old man took an iron grip on the intruder's wrist and made his favourite move, moving the hand round and facing it into the man's stomach. Since the guy happened to be still holding a gun, there was no surprise that it went off with a small sigh. The man sagged immediately, going down at the knees.

The man behind, although there for support, wasn't quick enough to realise what was going on, or to take evasive action. Before he had time to take a breath, he was shocked to see a gun appear in his face - a pistol prised from the hand of his partner - and then it went off. Everything went black after that.

Mickey's Dad reached for the dying man and pulled him into the room, flinging him onto the bed.

Then he stepped past him and closed the door, quietly. He listened. There was no sound of movement outside.

He snapped a light on. He had been expecting it, and was able to avert his eyes. The man on the floor wasn't, and was dazzled. He had a screaming pain in his gut and he was temporarily blinded. He was at a disadvantage.

Mickey's Dad got into his face.

"Who sent you?" he hissed.

The man tried to look up, but he was disorientated and confused. He tried to lie.

"I don't know," he said. "Don't know. I was commissioned. Don't know."

"Wrong answer," Mickey's Dad told him, and shot the man in the leg with his own gun.

The indignity of the situation didn't seem to bother the intruder. The pain did. He tried to fight it.

"Don't know," he pleaded. "Stop. Stop!"

Mickey's Dad scanned the face. It wasn't familiar. One thing was sure, it wasn't the man who had tried to have a go at him in the hospital. No, not that man. Someone else. Some other assailant. Another enemy.

"Let's try again," he told the assassin. "I'm not going to give you many more chances."

The old man considered. This guy was all in black - so, prepared - but he had no face mask. Surely he would want to hide his identity from CCTV cameras and possible witnesses. That would be standard practice.

Unless, he was confident. Unless he knew that no one would betray him, even if he was seen?

Mickey's Dad thought about that. It narrowed the possibilities.

"One more time," he said. "I'll ask and you answer. Get it?"

The man was nodding, but he had his hands on his stomach and seemed to be doing his best to press in, maybe to staunch the blood flow. Right, he still thought he had a chance of getting out alive.

Time to stifle his hope, Mickey's Dad was thinking.

He was close, but not too close that he could be grabbed. He looked down at the man and waved his gun at him.

"Who sent you?"

"Don't know. Really, I don't - "

"Wrong answer."

Mickey's Dad shot the man in his other leg.

It wasn't a logical thing to do. The man had already lost a lot of blood. He would surely be in shock right now, and would probably go unconscious any moment. If he didn't get help soon, he would surely die.

Well, he will, the old man decided, standing up. No, I'm not waiting for an answer.

He was annoyed. Attempts on his life had that effect. He wasn't sympathetic.

Mickey's Dad looked around. He had already wiped his prints from the surfaces. He hadn't used the door handles without a handkerchief. He had a small bag in the bottom of the wardrobe. All he needed to do was pick that up -

When the police arrived, called in the morning, they would find two bodies and a shot-up bed. Making enquiries, they would find out who was using the room that night - the intended victim. He registered. He was a regular. They would get a name. It would be a name, but it wouldn't be Mickey's Dad's name. He'd been careful, and avoided that.

The man stirred on the floor. He was mumbling, through the blood dripping from his mouth.

Mickey's Dad knelt down, amazed that the man was trying to communicate. It wouldn't help him, of course. Even if he said something useful, the old man was past the point of caring what happened to the guy. He wouldn't save him.

The man said, whispering hoarsely: "Russians."

*   *   *   *   *

The next morning, the Verger arrived bright and early to clear up after the homeless people.

He was surprised to find them still there, enjoying a late breakfast.

"What are you doing here?" he asked, not aggressively. He was his usual jovial self.

"What are you?" a woman with a teapot demanded. "You aren't on the rota."

"I like to help."

"You get in the way," she snapped, and moved on, serving people who really deserved a cup of tea.

The Verger, not a man to be put off, took a seat on one of the benches - having poured his own cuppa - and started chatting to the church's 'guests'. He was a strong supporter of the Parish Council's decision to open the place up and provide sleeping space. He felt it was his Christian duty to be accommodating. He said he read it in the Bible.

He liked to hear people's stories.

They didn't give him any.

After several frustrating false starts, the verger started getting a little suspicious. Why didn't these individuals have any tragedies to relate? What about failed marriages, bankrupt businesses, bereavements, Mental Health issues?

They had nothing.

Then what the Hell - pardon me, Lord - the man was thinking, were they doing there?

Confronted by his uncharitable feelings, the Verger took himself into the kitchen and busied himself with washing up and putting away for nearly an hour. He liked to see the surfaces spotless. It took all of his attention.

When he'd reached a natural break, he went back into the socialising area. The benches were empty, and the tables had been wiped and cleared. He smiled in approval at that. Finally, we've finished for another night.

Then he heard voices coming from the workroom.

No! he was thinking. No, this isn't right.

We had an agreement - the arrangement, as laid out to the Parish Council, was that the homeless would not arrive before seven in the evening and would be gone by ten the next day. That meant the building was free for all the other activities that this local church enjoyed during daylight hours - Sewing, Kurling and Bingo included.

That couldn't happen if the meeting rooms were occupied.

It was so unfair! We give them a bed, he thought furiously, but they need to give us back our building.

We didn't ask them to become 'Squatters'!

He was angry now, and ready to give some people a 'piece of his mind'. The Verger had a strong sense of Fair Play. He hated people 'taking advantage'. He was a very old-fashioned sort of man, and he was proud of it.

The Verger stomped across the room and threw open the door to the workroom, ready for a fight.

He stopped, speechless.

All the people he had seen previously - Yes, none of them had gone, vacated the premises. They were still there, and they were sitting either side of the big table. Some were sewing, some were -

It was hard to make sense of what they were doing. They seemed to be packing rucksacks. With - things. All kinds of things, like old clothes, and clocks, and wires. It seemed completely nonsensical. He was baffled.

"What are you doing here?" a voice said, behind him.

The old man turned. It was the Vicar, the lady Priest. She looked put out to find him there, so unexpected.

He wanted a word.

He pulled the door closed, gripped her elbow and pulled her back towards the kitchen.

"We agreed," he said fiercely, "that the homeless would leave - early in the morning."

"They aren't homeless."

The Verger took a step back. She knew! Whatever it was, this mystery - she had the answer.

The Vicar led him back into the kitchen, opened a cupboard and pulled out the coffee percolator.

The Verger sighed. This is a bad sign. She's getting out the good stuff. She's getting ready to break Bad News.

He was told to sit down. The coffee arrived, was stirred and poured out. The Vicar relished the taste.

"What are they doing?" the Verger demanded. He wanted a reply, on behalf of the Parish Council.

"They are - Well, what would you call them? - they are 'Terrorists', I suppose," she said. "They come here in the evening and sometimes work all night. They stuff rucksacks and make fake bombs. It's a campaign."

"Bombs!"

"Fake bombs. They aren't real. They are 'suspicious packages', and are left on trains, and buses, and trams. It causes consternation, ties up the Security Services and inconveniences travellers. Nobody dies."

"And you let them do it?" the Verger hissed. "Have you lost your mind?"

The Vicar took a breath. She took a sip of coffee.

"I've lost my faith," she said at last, admitting the inevitable. "We can't rely on God to make this world a better place. Those people, the ones in there, are dedicated to improving things for the better, that's why I trust them."

The Verger shook his head, despairingly. "If the Bishop hears about this - " he gasped.

"What? I'll lose my job? Don't worry, I'll have lost my life by the time that happens."

The Verger felt tears in his eyes. What was she saying? No, he couldn't lose her!

The lady Vicar said: "I've got cancer. I'm dying. I don't know how long I've got left. Maybe I'll make it to Christmas."

"You've got to fight it!" the man said. "You can't give up. We need you!"

The Vicar put her hand on top of the Verger's hand, where it rested on the table. She wanted to be reassuring.

"I've had the best advice," she told him. "I've been offered the best treatment. Nothing is going to work."

"Jeremy's device!" the Verger said, grasping at straws. "He says he can cure this stuff, right? Well, what have you got to lose? Try that. Try anything. I think I speak for the whole congregation when I say - "

"Don't say it," she told him, and there were tears coming from her too. ""Don't. You don't have to speak. I think I know what our little family would say. I know how they feel, I really do, and I'll be sorry to leave them."

"We have to buy one of those - those - "

She laughed out loud.

"I bought one," she said. "The first week he came here. As soon as I saw it, I bought one. It's in my office, in my desk. I put it in a drawer, and I haven't taken it out. It's still in its box, still in its wrapping. I haven't tried it. Not once."

He didn't say anymore. He just finished his coffee, stood up and extended a hand. She took it, as if glad of the support. They went out of the kitchen and across the hall to her office. They both knew what they were looking for.

Me? the Vicar was thinking to herself. Not me. I didn't think I would be ever doing this.

Not ever.

* * * * *

Later that morning, Terry was in his workroom, laughing to himself.

His research had paid off. He'd found exactly what he needed, and it was making him smile, hugely.

In fact, Two Things.

The first was that he'd found dirt on his Deputy Director, the hateful Mr Richard Caulfield.

The first bit had been an accident.

Terry had several 'traces' set up, changes in status that would trigger an alert on his system. The first one was about membership of The Sacred Society. He'd been forced to do it. After the government Review of 2015, following the General Election, it was agreed that any employees of British Security that were already members of the Society would be allowed to maintain their status. However, no new staff would be allowed to join.

Caulfield had transgressed that ruling. He had knowingly - some might say, willingly - applied and had his application accepted, and had been seen by members of the North West group at meetings of the Society.

They had reported it to Captain Gibson's office, which meant it was seen by Terry.

It was too, too perfect!

Terry knew what Caulfield thought, because he had often mentioned it, that he felt left out - excluded - by the fact he had never been in The Sacred Society. He thought it had brought problems his way. He also thought - presumably - that if he rectified that problem, by joining, all his former difficulties would be over. In fact, since the rules had now been changed. the fact that he wasn't in before but was in now, was precisely the thing that would make life difficult now.

But there was more.

People in London had heard about Mr Caulfield's heroic escapades with rucksacks, and sent Mr Gibson, the boss of operations in the North West, a memo to see that they would be delighted to see footage of Caulfield 'in action'.

Terry was delegated to trawl through the CCTV and see what video he could cobble together from all Richard's recent adventures. Terry was a little sceptical - when he saw the coverage, he was confirmed in his fears.

Caulfield didn't look good on camera. His reports might have painted him in a 'heroic' light, but the camera didn't lie. In 'real life' Mr Caulfield looked terrified. No, worse. Scared. Nervous. Fearful. Panicking.

The stories bandied about in the canteen and repeated around the water coolers of the Unit weren't backed up with evidence. Richard Caulfield looked like the most unlikely and undeserving 'hero' in the Unit, ever.

Which was true.

Terry chortled his way through a lot of video. It made him laugh outright. This was Caulfield all right, the 'real' Caulfield.

In some ways it showed him to be the marshmallow he was, and Terry felt a little bit sorry for him. But he wasn't going to let those emotions get in his way. When he turned in the tapes, Terry knew, Caulfield would be in big trouble.

Terry was ready for that. He would stick it to the Deputy Director. He had decided. He was going to be ruthless.

While he waited for his boss, Mr Gibson, to call for the completed compilation though, Terry busied himself on other matters.

He didn't take him long to think about that, well, 'incident' that had happened in Bury. The problem he had suffered with the van driver, the red van, and the aggressive way he had been treated. Terry wasn't usually vindictive, but the use of CCTV gave him an idea. He started checking to see if there were any cameras around a certain roundabout.

He couldn't be as precise as that.

No, he couldn't find any record of the actual confrontation, but Terry found footage of the van - the red van - approaching the turn-off, and also returning onto the motorway, on that day in question. That gave him one tremendous advantage: Terry could freeze the frame and blow it up, for a close-up shot.

It gave him the registration number of the van.

He then ran that through the vehicle archive records and he came up with the name and address of the vehicle keeper. It was the man he had seen on the road, the same lunatic who had jumped out of the van and waved his fist at Terry.

Then Terry did something really unusual - for him. He took revenge.

Terry ran the man's name and address through police databases, as well as the Local Authority. He found that the man had a pile of outstanding parking tickets and speeding fines against his name. He flagged them, which pushed the man's identity to the top of the list for police attention. In the next few days, Terry was thinking, the driver would be getting a knock on his door. The police would have a warrant, and would want to get the man into court to answer for his crimes.

There was more.

The man was self-employed, a sole trader, and he hadn't filed a Tax Return for years. Well, her Majesty's Tax Office couldn't follow up on all the infringements, but again, Terry put a hustle on it, marking the case 'Urgent'. That meant that of all the thousands of people with outstanding issues, this particular red van driver would be taken seriously.

Terry sighed. He wasn't proud of himself but he wanted to prove a point.

He was young. He was thin. He wouldn't do well in a stand-up fight. But there was more than one way of winning an argument, and Terry had found one. The van driver, so stroppy, so willing to use his fists, would find that he couldn't stand up to the combined forces of the State - when prompted into action by a skilled computer nerd.

There was a knock on the door, and Terry's train of thought was once more interrupted.

It was Melia. Again.

"Yes, come in, come in," Terry said, clearing a space for her and moving all his reports and print-outs aside.

"You wanted to see me?" Melia said, smiling brightly.

Terry looked at her admiringly. He loved Melia, he was thinking. In his own way. It wasn't flashy, but it was real.

"Mr Caulfield has been tasked with looking through your history," Terry said, clearing his throat.

He's looking for compromising material, he told her. He's trying to embarrass you.

"Well, Good News," Terry said. "I've got up stuff on him. We can do a swap. I'll keep my material undercover if he does the same. It's not like blackmail, not really. But it is a Threat. I can threaten him. He'll have to back off."

Melia smiled at him. "That's sweet," she said generously. "But really, what's the point?"

"So he won't give you a bad report!" Terry said, enthusiastically. "If we let him, he could completely ruin your chances of getting Captain Gibson's job of Director. I'll block

Caulfield and he won't be able to block you. Your way will be clear to getting the top job! It may not be immediate, of course, but the way will be clear."

"Thanks, Terry," she said, putting a hand on his.

Electricity ran through his body. He suddenly felt himself again. Alive.

"You're nice," she told him. "You've always supported me and I appreciate it, I really do."

But? There was a big 'but' coming soon, Terry could feel it.

"I've made up my mind," Melia said, and he was the first to know. "I don't want to be Director. I've decided."

10. CHAPTER NINE: News and Goodbyes

The next day, Captain Gibson was sitting next to Mickey's Dad in the Oncology Clinic waiting room at Salford Hospital.

They were both there to get progress reports on the current state of their various diseases.

Gibson, in particular, wasn't feeling optimistic that he would be getting any welcome news. He hadn't be feeling well recently, and it wasn't just the side effects of his medication, he concluded. He had a succession of pains below his rib cage. It was easy to believe, he was thinking, that his guts were failing, just ceasing to function effectively.

Mickey's Dad had problems with his throat and chest, he knew that too. From the start, he had co-operated with the Doctors, right from when he first realised he had problems, but nothing had cleared the shadow from the X-rays. There was something there, something deadly, and no medicine was going to shift it now, he was thinking.

They were both gloomy, both negative. A terrible depression had settled over them. There seemed no hope.

"That's another thing we've got in common," Mickey's Dad said, with a sad smile.

He was referring to the fact that Gibson had greeted him with the line, 'That's one thing we have in common', when the man mentioned he was Mickey's Dad. Yes, they had Mickey in common. Yes, they both worried about him.

Right then, neither had any clear idea where Mickey was or what he was doing. Not even Gibson, who was nominally Mickey's boss. But the latest assignment had been fed to

Mickey directly from Head Office in London and Gibson hadn't been involved. That sometimes happened - the Big Brass went over his head.

Previously, when such a thing happened, Gibson went to Terry and said something like, 'Can you keep an eye on him?' and Terry had complied. If there was a problem, the Director would be told. That was as far as it went.

In fact, the two old men were getting on surprisingly well. They had been meeting up regularly since that first meeting. Old soldiers, they could occupy whole evenings in active reminiscing - and drinking, that was their forte.

They enjoyed each other's company.

Either would be sad if the other died, they knew that, but their professional lives had involved losing a lot of colleagues over the years. It would be sad, but it wouldn't be surprising. The other would raise a glass to their fallen pal, and move on. Life would continue. For Gibson, there was a further reason for depression, though. In some ways the worst thing wouldn't be just getting ill, and dying. It would be carrying on living - and losing his job.

No longer Director of his Unit - would he want to 'carry on', or would he want life to end, anyway?

A nurse came out and called for Mickey's Dad. The old man rose, a little unsteadily, grinned at Gibson and went.

Like last time - for no obvious reason - he was taken into a cubicle and told to undress. They laid him back on a makeshift bed, wearing nothing but a hospital gown, and administered a drug that made him sleepy.

Mickey's Dad felt his eyes opening and closing. Every time they opened, someone different was in the space.

The knife man was a surprise.

Is this a dream? he wondered, or simply a memory of that previous attempt - the fake 'Muffin' man?

Was it someone different? The guy was tall, dressed in a white coat. He had a hunting knife in his hand.

Then he got closer, and Mickey's Dad's heart skipped a beat. No, it was the same man! The fake!

The pretend 'Martin Muffin' leaned over his victim. He had a huge grin on his face. Well, I tried and failed, he seemed to be saying, but look at me now - I'm back for a second try, and this time, it's going to work.

The curtain shifted behind him, and a second man stepped into the cubicle.

The assailant had no idea who he was. He simply didn't recognise Captain Gibson, Director of TEEF.

They had never met.

Gibson was standing next to a tray of surgical instruments. There was a line of different size scalpels.

He didn't seem to move, but something happened, and, a moment later, there was a steel scalpel sticking out of the attacker's arm, above the wrist and below the elbow. His knife wobbled.

The faker looked down at the blade. He was puzzled. He hadn't seen anything happen, it was so quick.

Before he had time to come to a conclusion, a second scalpel hit him, above the elbow.

Now that hurt! he was thinking.

He felt blood dripping down his arm. The white coat was running with rivulets of red. He felt unsteady on his feet.

I'm no pin cushion! 'Mr Muffin' was screaming in his thoughts, but the assault continued. More scalpels.

The huge knife suddenly seemed too heavy to hold, and it fell to the floor with a crash. It was getting too tiring to stand, the man was thinking, and felt himself staggering backwards. His knees came up against the bed.

"You are suffering from blood loss and shock," Captain Gibson told him formally. "You had better surrender and accept medical assistance before your systems shut down and you are past saving."

The attacker slipped unceremoniously to the floor, his head reeling. He couldn't think, could hardly breathe.

"What on Earth is going on in here?" an imperious voice declared.

Gibson turned. An officious older man in white coat had entered. He was clutching a large brown envelope.

The Captain introduced himself and described how he was attempting to save Mickey's Dad's life.

"So am I," the consultant said testily, and waved his envelope.

"I have some good news for you," he went on, talking to the man in the bed. "You have made improvements."

Mickey's Dad tried to focus. The Doctor was speaking to him? There was something he was trying to say?

"If you don't mind," the consultant said to Gibson, "I need to talk to my patient. Perhaps you would be so good as to leave us. Perhaps you could also summon assistance for this body on the floor. The Police may need to be called."

Gibson found himself grinning, happy at the good news for his new friend.

He hesitated. "Do you think it's anything to do with his recent treatment?" he asked, anxious for an answer.

He meant the ultrasound treatment, the device being peddled by Jermy Cermoney that they had both tried.

The Doctor was thinking of the chemotherapy that he had prescribed. He had never had great faith in it.

He shrugged. "People get ill, they get better," he said, not really clear that he was free to talk to his man with the moustache about his patient, the man in the bed. Still he couldn't stop giving an opinion.

"It happens," he said. "Sometimes it happens, anyway. Whatever you do."

* * * * *

Caulfield was not enjoying his day with the Bomb Squad.

I never should have accepted their invitation, he was thinking to himself. I was being foolish.

But he was flattered.

The man who had talked to him on the phone that day in the Mayor's office, invited Caulfield to come down and 'meet the team'. They were a great bunch of lads. Based at an old police station in the centre of town, they greeted him warmly and made him feel welcome. They sat with him in their canteen and shared stories.

"You did a good job," one of them said to their guest. "Not everyone could have stayed so calm."

It was that thing, the Deputy Director was thinking to himself, that thing about being 'a hero'. He liked that. He wanted it. He knew that most of these men (and a few women) had often been in life-threatening positions in their professional careers, and they had done what he'd done on the day - kept calm under pressure and followed orders.

"We get most of our training sitting in a classroom," an old hand said, sharing experience, "but then, sometimes, we take it out into the field. You should try it. Come with us for a day."

Is that why he was in a field now? Caulfield was thinking to himself. A real field, complete with grass and cows.

He couldn't really see the point. Maybe it was to 'up the pressure'. There was only so much you could do in a classroom, with a board and tables and chairs. It just wouldn't feel like 'the real thing'. Here, in the open air, there was the weather for one thing - the threat of rain - and the wind. Also the difficulty of using the radio, hearing what advice you were being given. Caulfield had been talked through the defusing process, but only when he was in a building, and it was quiet.

He'd never realised the world could be so noisy! There were aircraft flying overhead. They were near Barton Airport, he was thinking. Little planes were taking off and landing, continuously. It was a distraction.

The instructor had given a task to all the new recruits, but Caulfield was having trouble hearing him.

"There's bags all over the field," the man said, pointing off behind him. "I want you to go out, pick the first target you come to and make a start. They are all similar, but not the same. Make sure your radios are on and operating."

It was a day of Defusing. They were all expected to go out, armed with nothing more than a pair of pliers.

Caulfield moved forward. This is different, he was thinking. Most days, I am a Deputy Director, with a desk and a secretary. Here, I'm on my own. It's thrilling, in a way. Or should be.

Actually, he felt cold, and uncomfortable.

He didn't like the overalls they'd given him. They were scratchy. And the helmet obscured his vision.

"Tell me what you see," the voice in his earpiece crackled.

"There's wires connected to a central box," Caulfield told his instructor.

It was confusing him. In films and TV series, it was usually a choice. Say, a red and a green. Or maybe a blue and a black. Here, he was looking at a jumble of colours, and they all seemed important.

"Look for the battery," he was told.

Richard Caulfield, Deputy Director of the new unit, TEEF, was suddenly confronted with facts about himself that he didn't want to learn. One, he was clumsy. When it came to trying to sort wires, wearing the thick gloves they had given him, he couldn't arrange his fingers in a way that didn't make them overlap and get in the way.

Second, he was shaking.

This is ridiculous, he thought to himself. It's not a real bomb. It can't be! They've put together pieces of real-life stuff, like batteries and detonators, but they were blanks. Surely. He didn't really have anything to worry about!

Thirdly, he had no memory.

Not for this sort of stuff. Looking at one wire, say, the yellow, finding out where it went and what it was connected to. Then moving on to the red, following that down. It came to a terminal next to the yellow, near the round thing. Which was what? He had been told, only a few moments before, but he couldn't remember. Not the technical name, the thing that he had heard from the instructor. Was it a 'solenoid'? No, that was on the side. Or was it?

Richard Caulfield, slightly overweight, almost middle-aged, found that sitting on his haunches was uncomfortable. He switched to his knees, but after only a short time, they started to ache. He was getting cramp in his calf muscles.

Then, he found himself sweating, even though it was a Spring day, brisk and cold. Beads of sweat started coming down his forehead and getting into his eyes. He couldn't wipe them off unless he took off a glove.

Before long, he found himself getting irritated and flustered. I need to keep calm! he was thinking.

A hundred yards away, across the field and near the hedge, the Chief Instructor was listening in to the increasingly flustered talk of their star guest. He wasn't impressed. This man will never make the grade, he was thinking.

It wasn't making him happy. Firstly, he hadn't been content when his boss said that they were having a 'special guest' for the day. The man was a civilian! What did he know about explosives? It was a Publicity stunt. The guy had been in the Press - He had done something, somewhere. Well, journalists might be fawning, but it was nothing to him.

Secondly, it put him in an impossible position with the Society.

He knew that Caulfield was a member - they had shaken hands - and the Chief Instructor knew his duty. In the normal course of events, he would have been prepared to do whatever was needed for a Brother. But Caulfield was hopeless! He couldn't pretend! No, there was no way this day was going to end happily. He would have to admit, to whomsoever wanted to know, that the wonderful Mr Caulfield had failed his assessment. Unfortunately. The Chief Instructor wanted to be helpful, but he couldn't make cheese out of chalk. They were entirely different substances. His team were made of sterner stuff. The guest was nothing more than an inflated ball of fluff.

He was no hero, that was for sure.

* * * * *

Later that day, in the evening, Mickey's Dad went to see Melia, in her flat.

She wasn't expecting him. In fact, she didn't know he was in Manchester. Even though the man had met Terry, the team's technician, and Mr Gibson, the unit's Director, neither had got round to sharing with their gorgeous colleague the fact that her boyfriend's father had arrived in the area for a visit.

Perhaps the two men were waiting for 'the right time', They were both highly protective of Melia. Maybe they'd thought it through and realised it would be unsettling for her. But, unfortunately, putting it off like that, it meant that when the old man arrived on Melia's doorstep, it was even more of a shock that if she had been - even slightly - forewarned.

"Come in, Come in," Melia said, waving her guest towards a comfy chair. "A drink?" she said. "What can I get you?"

Mickey's Dad stood near the couch. He was breathing heavily.

It had been a difficult day.

Melia stopped, seeing how uncomfortable he seemed.

"Are you all right?" she asked slowly, concerned.

His grizzled face broke out in a huge grin.

"I'm fine," he said, paused and added: "I'm better than fine."

He sat down then.

"Melia, I came to Manchester because I thought I would be saying goodbye. I'd been told I had cancer and it wouldn't take long to finish me off. Today, at the hospital, they told me it was fading. I don't know why. I don't care. It means I have a few years left, and I'm going to make the most of them. I've still got a lot of travelling to do."

Melia suddenly felt tears in her eyes.

"You aren't going to wait? To see Mickey?"

His Dad looked sympathetic, but he wasn't smiling at that.

"He can come and find me, any time he wants to," the old man said.

Melia found her breath coming in gasps. She couldn't make sense of any of it!

"I don't know where he is!" she said, her voice cracking. "I don't know when he's coming back. I worry about him."

Mickey's Dad stood up.

"That's one thing we have in common," he said.

He took her in his arms. He was a big man, and the hug was reassuring.

Melia didn't move until her breathing returned to normal, and her anxiety calmed down. She felt better, just the way she did when she was in Mickey's arms. These men had a lot about them that was similar, she realised.

They went into Melia's kitchen and she showed the old man her wine cupboard. He took out a few bottles and read the labels. He seemed to know what he was doing. After some humming and hawing, he picked a French red.

He went back into the living room, took off his coat and slung it over a chair and sat back down on the settee. He opened the bottle with a corkscrew and let the wine breathe for a while. He was in no rush.

Melia fussed around, bringing out plates and glasses. She found some cheese in the fridge, and biscuits in the other cupboard. She arranged the nibbles on a tray and put them on the low coffee table.

Now, what were they going to talk about?

"He's never mentioned you," Melia said, a little uneasily.

Mickey's Dad chuckled. "Sometimes I imagine that he'd like to think he was some kind of orphan," he said. "In fact, when he was at school, I think he told some of his chums just that! He's never been proud of me, unfortunately."

Melia stared at the man. "But he copied you!" she said. Mickey was an agent, just like his Dad.

"We never listen to what our parents say," the old man said calmly, "but we often simply do what they did."

Melia wasn't sure what to say.

She knew she could have asked the man what he'd been doing recently, and if he'd had any exciting moments. But she also knew that he probably wouldn't have been able to tell her much. That was the nature of their lives. There was stuff they could share, and stuff they couldn't. She had come to appreciate that, over the years.

Mickey's Dad poured the wine, sampled it, licked his lips approvingly and shared it.

"It's best I don't stay around here," he said amiably. "There are a number of people who seem hell bent on killing me. A couple have come close in the last few weeks. I don't know what it is, I just seem to upset people."

"Anyone I know?"

Mickey's Dad thought about that. Yes, it was possible, he realised. The last pair were paid assassins, working for a Russian oligarch that he had managed to cross. It was conceivable the same men could have targetted Melia.

"As soon as I knew about you," Mickey's Dad said, without saying how he'd heard about her, or from whom, "I worried that you'd never have a proper relationship with my son. You're both living in the same dangerous world. How could you ever create a family life? You know, Melia, I've thought about that. I really would like grandchildren."

Melia found herself becoming sad again. Sure, she was thinking, maybe I shared that dream. Once.

In fact, in the last few years, she had come close. She had found herself pregnant recently, but lost the baby.

"That would be nice," she agreed, trying not to sound too morbid. "If only it were possible."

"Everything's possible, Melia. We both know that. You just have to want it hard enough."

They drank more wine and talked about Mickey. That was safe ground, the secrets and memories they could share.

Melia even began to talk about herself. The old man seemed genuinely interested, and listened intently. He wanted to get to know this lady, the potential daughter-in-law he'd never had. There was an unfulfilled longing in him for a family, a real live bunch of people who might care for him and involve him in their continuing lives.

He'd never had that.

"I'd better be going," Mickey's Dad said at last, putting down his wine glass.

"You could stay."

He looked at her. They both knew that if he was in her flat, he was putting her at risk.

She had thought of that. "I have a key to the top flat," she told him. "Donald is away and I'm feeding his fish. You could sleep up there. Even if anyone has followed you here, they won't realise you're elsewhere in the building."

Mickey's Dad was grateful, knowing that he'd only have to play 'hide and seek' with hotels in Manchester if he didn't take Melia's offer. Or, he was thinking, she could sleep upstairs - safe - and if anyone crashed in on him, down here, he could deal with them, as he had done before. Either way, they needed to look after each other.

They both stood up, still considering the options. They hadn't made up their minds.

"You know," Melia said, her mind going off on another thought, "I've never even asked you your name."

"Mickey."

She stared. That didn't seem right. Was HER Mickey, a sort of 'Junior' then?

"His name isn't Mickey," his Dad said.

Melia was shocked. She had known the younger man - how long? But she'd never even known his real name?

"His name is Darnley," his Dad said. "It was his mother's idea. She's Scots, and obsessed with Elizabeth the First, Queen of England in Shakespeare's day. The name comes from that time. They used to call him 'Dan' at school."

Melia had been feeling tense, wound up, and this latest revelation seemed to open a door. It certainly opened flood gates, Tears streamed down her face, and she found herself racked with spasms of grief.

Her life was such a mess! She couldn't believe she had got herself into this predicament. How had it happened?

Mickey's Dad stepped forward and held her again, standing in for his son, who wasn't there.

11.   CHAPTER TEN: A place in the sun

Several days later, Captain Gibson went to visit his son in prison.

It was a disappointment to the parent to see his offspring languishing behind bars, but the biggest disappointment was the inane and indefensible reason for him being there.

"Drugs," Gibson said to his adopted charge. "Did it have to be so stupid?"

"Take it easy, Dad," the kid said, slumping across the table in the Rec Room where families were allowed to meet their relatives. David seemed to having trouble speaking. He was slurring his words, and finding it hard to focus.

"Are you high now?" the Captain asked incredulously. Were drugs that easy to get inside?

The son looked at his father patronisingly. Did the old man know nothing? Did he live in the Real World?

Gibson leaned forward and his voice was insistent.

"If you're in here," he said, "you can't be looking after you daughter! She needs you, David. Don't you know that?"

"I'm paying someone - " he said, then lost the thread, unable to finish the sentence.

"Social Services have her," Gibson told him.

The son looked mildly surprised. He had left his child in the care of a neighbour. He didn't know that when the authorities came round for a 'routine' visit, they found the 'caretaker' insensible, with a needle sticking out of their arm. The visitors took the child away immediately.

The Captain tried to explain these circumstances, but it merely confused the boy.

He had money, he said.

Yes, Gibson knew that. He had asked Terry to do some checking, and the technician reported to his boss that there had been a sudden and massive improvement in the kid's bank balance. Terry's algorithms also alerted him to the fact that David had been caught in a drugs swoop and was being held on remand. Gibson decided to visit.

He took the precaution of taking Terry with him. When there was no reply at the flat door - and no interest from any of the nearby flats - Gibson ordered Terry to break in. He managed to get through the lock without actually 'breaking' it.

They found a mess, including drug paraphernalia. They knew it would only be a matter of hours before the Police came round and did their own search, so they did a sweep. They found drugs, of course, and flushed what they could down the toilet. They also found a rucksack in a wardrobe that contained the other half of the ransom that the Metro Mayor had paid - the money that Caulfield has so unskilfully lost. Gibson insisted on 'looking after it'. He didn't hand it in.

"Cash," David mumbled, still unsteady enough not to be able to balance his hand on his hand and his elbow on the table at the same time. He made several attempts, but he keep slipping, and almost tumbled straight onto the floor.

"Yes, I know about that," his father told him.

Gibson had no intention of giving the money back, and he certainly wasn't going to hand it in in any way that would implicate his ward. He owed him that much anyway. If you couldn't circumvent Law and Order once in a while, Gibson was thinking, what was the point of being a custodian of justice? His judgement would have to do.

Anyway, money wasn't a problem.

"I've found a buyer for the house in London," Gibson explained, not sure whether he was understood, or even heard. He ploughed on. "I'll be putting your share of the proceeds into your bank, using a simple electronic transfer. When you get out of here, and sober up, you should be able to get hold of it, as much as you need, whenever you need it."

"Thanks, Dad."

The Captain looked at the young man. Did he just thank him? Did he understand what he was saying?

The point is, the Captain wanted to say, we all deserve a second chance.

You, David, can then get out of that hell hole, maybe find a better flat somewhere, and maybe start your life again. You won't have to get a job - straight away - and you can take your time to think about what you really want to do.

Me, David, I've got a second chance too.

It was true. The Consultant at the hospital had called him in for an 'urgent' appointment. Gibson feared the worst, thinking it was bad news, but it was quite the opposite. Just as with Mickey's Dad before him, he was told that he had made 'massive and unexpected' improvements. His tumour had shrunk. There was no evidence of any spread into other organs or tissue, and his blood count was approaching normal. It was all good. He could go back to work.

Ah, that was the awkward part. Captain Gibson wasn't sure he had any job to go back to, so he was surprised, one cold night, when his phone rang at his Salford house and a cold voice informed him that the Minister wanted to talk.

There was a click and the woman came on the phone.

Gibson felt he had nothing to lose. He related his medical woes. He reported how close he had come to disaster.

"But you're better now?" the clipped voice commented. Gibson said yes. "Good. We need you."

The Captain had no idea what manoeuvrings had been going on down in London, but strangely, he was back in favour. If he could 'see his way clear' to taking up the reins again, the job was his, he was told. Gibson gave a huge sigh of relief. He was well aware - thanks to his informant Terry - how difficult the struggle had been to find his successor, and the reluctance of anyone trustworthy to step forward to take his place.

Terry also said, in the spirit of complete honesty, that the vacuum in the chain of command had brought out the worst in Deputy Director Caulfield, and he was taking pleasure in humiliating Melia. Gibson wasn't going to stand for that.

Once he'd been told his post was secure, the first thing he did was dash off a note to Terry. 'I'll see you all next Monday', it said. 'Please get everyone to step back into line.'

Gibson felt gratified to be given yet one more chance. I will do well, by everyone, he vowed.

There is no need for me to retire, he was thinking. Not right now. Another day, maybe, but not today.

Well, that was more or less a happy ending. Good for him, for Terry, for Melia, even for Caulfield, if he did but know it.

No, the only loser out of the whole sorry episode was David's daughter.

Gibson had sought medical advice. He knew people, he could pull strings. People at the hospital dived into her file for him and checked out the ongoing treatment and range of possible prognoses. Then they reported back.

It was all Doom and Gloom. Not one doctor held out any hope at all. It was just a matter of time, they said.

Gibson looked down at the drugged-up mess that was his adopted son, and felt so, so sorry for the boy. One day soon he would come down from his illegal high and crash and burn. His whole life would fall apart. He had lost his wife, his girlfriend, his friends and colleagues, and now he would lose his daughter.

Well, the boy kept saying he didn't want my help - apart from repeated subs of small sums of money, mainly for drugs - but this time it's different, the old man decided. I'm going to stick by him, every step of the way. He will have me to pick him up and put him back on the straight and narrow. I will stay with him, for as long as I've got left in this life.

I'm a parent, Gibson decided. No one ever said it was an easy job, or that anyone - anyone - would ever thank you for the efforts you put in. Tough. He would be going that extra mile, and every footstep and yard needed. From now on.

For ever.

* * * * *

On the evening of that day, Melia was waiting in her flat for an expected visitor.

Gorange.

Melia didn't know how long this could go on. The man had been a regular caller. They had spent many hours together. The fact was, as they both acknowledged, they enjoyed each other's company. It was fun.

It would be fun - until he died.

There was no doubt about that, he told her. He had come back to England to see her - that was a given - but also to see medical experts. His diagnosis of cancer had been made in a desert kingdom, a place where the level of expertise could not be counted on. Gorange didn't need Harley Street, he told her, but he needed someone in a clean coat.

He found that person, obviously, even in the far north of England. Manchester had experts, he said, and they told him. Nothing could save him. The disease was in his bones. He was being eaten alive, from the inside out.

Well, the days were ticking away. The terrorist was looking more gaunt and haggard every day, but he had always been lean, stick-like. He wasn't short, but was thin. How could she know if he was losing weight? It didn't show.

That wasn't the only countdown, of course. The clock of heaven, ticking away the remaining minutes of Gorange's life, would also be marking another deadline - the day and minute that Mickey arrived back at her door.

Melia sighed. Which would come first, a death, or a confrontation that could signal the finale of her romance?

They were both endings.

Her doorbell buzzed, and she went out onto the landing, outside the door to her flat. She could see down the stairs to the front door. Someone was coming in. There was talk, some laughing. The front door to the building slammed shut and a couple started up towards her. They looked drunk, careless and carefree. It was noisy.

It was the girl who lived in the flat opposite, Melia was thinking. Some new boyfriend, perhaps? They appeared close, hanging on to each other. It would be rude to stare at them, Melia was thinking and started to step back.

It all happened at once.

The couple reached Melia's floor, the man threw the woman to one side and bundled Melia back through her door and onto the settee in her living room. He kicked the door closed behind him, and looked around.

It was a ruse, Melia realised. The man had used the other woman as cover, in order to get into the block without arousing suspicion. The woman was Asian, Melia realised. The man was too. Maybe they knew each other. Perhaps the girl was helping the man, assisting him to follow through on his mission. His job. His plan.

Because there would be something, Melia knew. She recognised the man. She'd been carrying a photo of him around.

He was the 'Asylum Seeker' she had been looking for when she went to St Cyprian's church.

Now here he was.

As large as life, and twice as ugly. Younger than her, probably stronger. She would have to be careful.

Finally, she thought, I have found out why he wanted to come back to the UK, and why he was posing as a Homeless Person.

He was undercover, looking for Gorange.

"Where is he?" the young man barked, after he had checked the bedroom and kitchen. "I want him."

That threw her. He didn't want her too? But she was the Secret Agent. She represented the British Establishment.

He saw her puzzled expression and laughed outright.

"I don't want you!" he said scornfully. "I'm here to finish the job I started on the man with the scarred face."

Gorange, yes. Only him. He wanted to hurt Gorange.

The fact that people wanted to kill Gorange shouldn't have been a surprise - he'd attracted plenty of enemies over the years - but it just seemed so inappropriate, given his present condition. Why didn't they just wait? It would be over soon enough. He was dying, she wanted to yell. Why not give him a small amount of time, considering he has so little left?

Melia's buzzer went again.

The kid waved her over to answer it. She moved, slowly, not wanting to show willing.

It was Gorange. Melia pressed the button which released the main door to the building. They could hear the sound of footsteps downstairs. The big front door slammed. Someone was coming up.

The young man, not bothering to say anything, carefully opened the door to Melia's flat and looked out and over the balcony. Melia was behind him, but he didn't seem to care about her. That was a mistake.

She ran the few steps from the living room and through the hall, then launched herself in a flying rugby tackle at the back of the young man. She hit him too high, and didn't manage to bring him down, but she carried him forward and he stumbled out and crashed onto the metal railing along the top of the staircase.

The force of her attack took the breath out of him, but he shook her off like an annoying pet, and she found herself flung against the door of the flat opposite. Maybe the woman will come out, Melia was thinking. She might want to inspect the damage she had helped cause. She might want to see how her friend, this young man, was doing.

Gorange was half way up the last flight of stairs, when he saw the man, and saw what was happening to Melia.

He screamed obscenities, mounted the last few steps in a flurry and tore into the younger man, knocking him off his feet and pinning him to the ground. He crashed a fist into the unlined young face, and made it ugly, for once.

The man was scrabbling for the pocket of his coat. Melia, behind him, thought he might have a gun in there. She dragged herself forward and tried to grab the man's fist. He battered her away, again, and succeeded in pulling out a small automatic handgun. Melia twisted on the floor and lashed out with a foot. The gun flew out of the man's hand.

Gorange, breathing heavily, pulled himself up by grabbing the banisters. He was quite clearly struggling, and out of condition. He was making heavy weather of this confrontation, Melia was thinking. He needed more energy.

The man skittered across the floor, following his weapon. Melia thought she had cleared it, but it was still within reach. He scooped it up, pulled himself up the wall and turned to face them both. The gun was in his hand, pointing at Melia.

"Keep out of this," the young man hissed, waving the pistol this way and that.

It might be, Melia remembered thinking afterwards, that he had no intention of hurting her, but the fact that the gun was now pointing at her, made her a possible target, even if accidentally. It infuriated Gorange. He screamed out a warning, and hurled himself forward, grabbing for the weapon. There was a shot, as the gun went off.

He tried to protect me, Melia thought helplessly, but it was the end for him.

Gorange spun off to the right, up against the balustrade, then slipped down it slowly. There was a massive patch of red on the front of his shirt, and his hand was grasping at it uselessly.

The young man seemed satisfied. He could see his intended victim was hit, and he appeared content.

"This is all I need," he said to Melia and lowered the gun.

Really? If, in his wildest dreams, he imagined he could intrude into Melia's life, and the place where she lived, gun someone down in her presence, and then simply walk away - he didn't know Melia very well.

Clearly he didn't. There was a look of the utmost surprise on his face when Melia came for him, barrelling across the hallway and slamming all her weight into him, in a body block that hit him from head to midriff.

It was just unfortunate for him, and further evidence of his lack of planning, that he happened to be standing at the top of the flight of stairs. Melia's attack caught him off balance, and he bounced back off the wall and out into space. He tumbled head over heels down the first flight, hit the wall down there, and took the next set of stairs too.

Melia didn't wait to see how his journey ended. She turned and knelt down beside her old adversary.

"Don't talk," she told him. "Let me see what we can do."

Gorange was smiling. He tried to lift a hand to her face. His gaze was tender, even as his breath faltered.

"We have travelled this road together," he mumbled, as he gasped for air. "So far. So far."

It had to be someone, Melia was thinking, but why that guy? She reproached herself. If I'd done a better job - If I'd been nicer to the lady Vicar, or maybe more thorough, or asked more questions, maybe I'd have got the kid before he got through and found Gorange.

Then it would have been someone else who finished him, she was thinking.

Because, the final irony, if this had been only a few short years ago - it might have been her.

* * * * *

A few months later, Jeremy Ceremony was walking along the sands of a Caribbean beach in summer.

He was on his way to a lazy breakfast, taking the short walk from his bungalow, as he was used to doing these days. It was his new life. No responsibilities, no struggles, no confrontations. Freedom, and enough money.

Yes, he had enough money. More than enough. Martin Muffin had paid him off.

As Jermy suggested. The thought had occurred to him the first time he met a 'Martin Muffin'. The fake one. You can use a 'stick or a carrot', he told the young man. A threat or a bribe, either will work. So, when the real Mr Muffin eventually met up with Mr Cermoney and asked him to 'cease and desist' his campaign of promoting ultrasound as a way of curing cancer, Jermy just grinned and said: "How much are you willing to pay?"

Not that he needed much cash, actually. The car crash that changed his life - and his visage - had given him a pay-out of millions in insurance. Safely deposited in a bank and invested in various securities, it provided him with a modest income, and that had kept him solvent for many years. His Financial Advisor had given him another idea.

"This would go a lot further in certain parts of the world," he mused.

They looked for a place together. Eventually they hit on an island in the West Indies. Certain beaches hosted huge hotels, casinos and playgrounds, but there were plenty of places off the beaten track, that were still lovely -

Just cheaper.

Jermy was able to buy a property - a one-storey house big enough for his needs – and still have enough wealth to guarantee a continuing income that would keep him in food and drink for the rest of his natural life. Since he had no interest in casinos, anyway, he was set. He sold everything back in Britain, picked up his roots and transferred his whole life abroad.

He had never been happier.

Of course, his mission was over too, as was every other part of his former life. The talks and demonstrations of his healing device came to an abrupt end. Strangely, he didn't miss it.

I've done my bit, he concluded. I've saved thousands of lives, he thought - a slight exaggeration - and the Muffin Institute will continue my work, (which it had no intention of doing. They had their own ideas).

Jermy scuffed his feet in the sand. He was still unsteady while walking, and a beach wasn't the ideal place for him to walk safely, but he relished the soft surface, the gentle breeze and the blazing sun.

"Good Morning, Manuel," he announced, pushing open the half-door into the cantina. "The usual."

The man behind the bar hurried over with a glass of ice water and a napkin. He was holding letters.

"Your post for today, Señor Sermy," he said, in a strangled accent. His English was good. His name wasn't 'Manuel'.

Jermy had his post delivered to the bar. It was easier than expecting a post person to tramp the beach to his out-of-the-way hideaway. It suited him. He didn't want urgent missives. He didn't intend to respond to begging letters.

Mr Ceremony started opening envelopes. There was an English newspaper on the next table. He leaned over and looked at the front page. Snow, he read. He smiled. What do I miss about England? The weather?

A figure came and sat down opposite him. At the same table? Jermy knew some people, but he wasn't that amiable.

"We meet again," the fake 'Martin Muffin' said smoothly.

He was holding a bottle and a pair of glasses.

"Let's drink together," he suggested.

"It's a bit early for me," Jermy said, his voice a little unsteady.

He was spooked. What did this man want? Why was he here? How had he found him, so many miles from home?

"I know, you're surprised to see me," the visitor said. "But, honestly, I'm a journeyman, a contractor. I go wherever the work takes me. Right now, I've been asked to find you, so here I am. Simple. Eat your toast."

The waiter had brought plates of toast and cheese. He looked at the new arrival with suspicion, but said nothing.

"Jeremy, mate," the new man said. "This doesn't have to be unpleasant. I'll pour us both a drink. One of the glasses will have poison in it. It won't have an immediate effect. You finish your meal, go back to your shack, maybe sleep it off. The likelihood is that you won't wake up. Ever. That's not so bad, is it? A suitable way to die?"

"Who's paying you?"

The man who had once pretended to be a Muffin spread his hands.

"I wish I could tell you," he said generously. "But honestly? I'm a Man of Mystery. I mean, the last time I was in England, I was stuck with knives by that nice Captain Gibson of the anti-terrorist Unit. They had to take me to hospital to stop the bleeding and darn the wounds. Still, I survived. What Gibson and all his friends didn't know - and haven't ever been told - is that I have Diplomatic Immunity. My contacts managed to get me out of your country and back to Switzerland. Then, a mere few weeks later, I was exchanged for some compatriots in a Russian spy-swap. So, here I am. Back in business."

Jermy was looking at his hands. He had a piece of toast in one of them, and a knife with butter in the other. On the table was a fork - for the cheese - and a spoon, for the marmalade. He should be enjoying this, he was thinking angrily. This is my favourite meal of the day, then this buffoon barges in -

The healer suddenly realised he was more than angry. He was furious. His life had had its ups and downs, he couldn't deny that, but the last few weeks had been magical. Moving to this lovely land, settling in, meeting people.

I'll be damned I'm going to give any of this up, he was thinking! For the first time in my life, I'm truly happy.

It was something worth fighting for.

In one succinct movement, Jermy dropped the toast, scooped up the fork and slammed it into the back of 'Mr Muffin's' hand, where it was lying on the table. Before the visitor could get out a scream, his attacker had used the knife - in his other hand - to pin Muffin's other hand to the thick wooden plank. He was immobilised.

Jermy slooshed the contents of the bottle that his assassin had brought with him into the glasses he provided, dashed round the table and started pouring the fluid into Muffin's mouth. Jermy yanked on the man's hair so that he screamed and opened his mouth wide. The victim coughed and spluttered but couldn't help swallowing.

Whichever is the poison, Jermy was thinking, he will get it. Not for me! Oh, no. I'm too clever for him.

As Jermy continued the assault, he was surprised to see extra pairs of hands appear beside him. The waiter, the barman, and several of the regulars who sat on stools by the bar, had joined in, and were actually helping their friend.

Jermy felt tears coming to his eyes. I've never had friends before, he was thinking.

JC's Cure for Cancer

The man who had been paid to finish the life of Jeremy Ceremony found himself overwhelmed, hopelessly outnumbered. He was hammered on the head until he lost consciousness, then thrown to the floor, his hands freed from their knife and fork restraint, and his body carried out to the back yard of the cantina.

"We will take care of everything, Mr Cermoney," the man called 'Manuel' assured him. "Please. Finish breakfast."

Fresh toast was brought. The bottle and glasses were removed. Jermy resumed the start to his day.

As he rescued the mail that had slipped to the floor in the melee, one Greetings card fell out of its envelope and into his palm.

The front said, 'Thank you' and there was the picture of a flower. Inside, it said, 'From Mickey'.

Jeremy Ceremony was puzzled. A frown creased his usually untroubled features.

Now, what did I ever do for him? he wondered.

12. THE END

13. ABOUT THE AUTHOR

What can you say about Mike Scantlebury -
that hasn't been whispered in corners already?
An insignificant amount.

He was born to two parents on a dairy farm in Hornchurch but moved to England when young, (and could speak). His family settled in the West Country, near a town called Marshland, where his father was employed as a cow Inspector. When cjecking udders became unpopular in the 1980s, Mike packed his ties and moved in with some poety friends in the nearby big city of Bristol. This is where he first got involved in the dancing tradition, wrote old songs, and became interested in nepotism.

You can find Mike Scantlebury on the internet.
Amazon and Kindle.

Here's Mike's Author Page on Amazon:
http://www.amazon.co.uk/Mike-
Scantlebury/e/B0088IX1J8/

It's @MikeScantlebury on Twitter and 'mikescantlebury99' on Facebook. And, surprise, 'mikescantlebury' on Linked In.

If you want to see Mike singing, try Youtube.
https://www.youtube.com/user/mikescantlebury

If all else fails, try him at home (knock on):
http://www.Salford.me/

Other Books by Mike Scantlebury

(Author of Scanti-Noir)

The Amelia Hartliss Mystery series

Book One: Poison Doctor
Book Two: Hartliss Running
Book Three: Prince William (At Olympics 2012)
Book Four: Con-Fusion
Book Five: Mayors' Tales
Book Six: Secret Garden Festival 2012
Book Seven: Kidnapping Cameron
Book Eight: Secret Garden 2013
Book Nine: Fresh Heir
Book Ten: The Golden Chip
Book Eleven: The Folksinger 2013
Book Twelve: Salford World War
Book Fourteen: Salford Trenches
Book Fifteen: Terror Beach
Book Sixteen: A Shot at Mayor
Book Seventeen: JC's Cure for Cancer

The Mickey from Manchester series

Book One: Black and White
Book Two: Off The Rails
Book Three: A Limp Piccolo
Book Four: Filling In
Book Five: New, Clear Future
Book Six: Housing Erases Debts
Book Seven: The Bone Key Curse
Book Eight: Multimedia (*BBC comes to Salford*)
Book Nine: Lucky Ignatius
Book Ten: Reverend Dumb
Book Eleven: Jennercide
Book Twelve: Lethal Election
Book Fourteen: Trumps A Mayor
Book Fifteen: Senctioned
Book Sixteen: 75 Years

Printed in Great Britain
by Amazon

46403724R00088